Carmi G. Cantrell

The Cantrell Family

A Biographical Album and History of the Descendants of Zebulon Cantrell

Carmi G. Cantrell

The Cantrell Family
A Biographical Album and History of the Descendants of Zebulon Cantrell

ISBN/EAN: 9783337098162

Printed in Europe, USA, Canada, Australia, Japan

Cover: Foto ©Raphael Reischuk / pixelio.de

More available books at **www.hansebooks.com**

THE

CANTRELL FAMILY

A BIOGRAPHICAL ALBUM AND HISTORY

OF THE

DESCENDANTS OF ZEBULON CANTRELL
THE IMMIGRANT

WITH DATA CONCERNING THE FAMILIES WHO HAVE ALLIED
THEMSELVES WITH THE CANTRELLS
BY MARRIAGE

COVERING THE PERIOD FROM 1700 TO 1898

COMPILED AND EDITED BY

CARMI G. CANTRELL

OF THE SEVENTH GENERATION

SPRINGFIELD, ILL.
ILLINOIS STATE REGISTER PRINTING HOUSE
1898

PREFACE.

"He only deserves to be remembered by posterity
Who treasures up and preserves the history of his ancestors.
Edmund Burke.

Fifteen months ago I commenced to gather material for Family Record, intending to make a small pamphlet, giving the births, deaths, marriages, etc., of our family. The picture idea was suggested by my brother, Dr. Cantrell, and I am, indeed, grateful to the many who have furnished the pictures of themselves and their friends for this work. The preparation of this work has indeed been a patience cultivator and at the same time there has been much pleasure connected with it. I confess I have a certain degree of pride, as I write these closing words, in view of the fact that this is the first record of any size that has ever been made of our family.

My father said many times he was going to take his grandfather's record, which you will find in this book, and bring it on down, but he died without carrying it out. Many others talked of this, but failed in doing it. Mr. Power says in his "Early Settlers of Sangamon County:" "It is surprising that there are not more families who write up their own histories. Family pride is commendable and viewed properly should be a powerful stimulus to right living, but it can have no reliable foundation without written history."

I caught the inspiration for this work largely from his book and acknowledge considerable help from it; still I have verified every fact from other sources. I can not account for the different spelling of the name. I am sure we are all one family. I have spelled the name in each case as directed. Although this work is not complete, and no doubt there are many mistakes in it, still it is the best I could do under the circumstances. If the members of the family will furnish me the material I will promise to add to this record at some future date.

CARMI G. CANTRELL.

Irvington, Ind., September, 1898.

EXPLANATION.

On page 2 of the Record you will find a copy of a Record made by Zebulon G. Cantrell. He was the oldest of nine sons, five of whom, Zebulon, Joshua, William G., Levi and Wyatt raised families. The first two of these men never had a picture taken. The Album begins with the large cuts of the three younger brothers, followed by the families in their order.

In the Record the names of the heads of these families are in large black letters, their children in capitals and their grandchildren in small capitals. Zebulon G.'s family is the first in the Record; Joshua's begins on page 23, William G.'s on page 35, Levi's on page 44 and Wyatt's on page 62.

From page 67 to the close you will find partial records of Thomas Cantrill's, Aaron Cantrell's and Thomas Cantrell's Family. Remembering the book is thus divided into families you will easily find any name.

Biographical Album

OF THE

Cantrell Family

WILLIAM G. CANTRALL.

John McCollam Cantrell.   Joanna M. Cantrell.

John M. Cantrell was born February 22, 1808, in Kentucky. His parents moved to Ohio. There he learned the blacksmith trade. November 18, 1830, he married Joanna M. Jones. She was born September 11, 1812. They moved to Sangamon county, Illinois, in 1831. In 1834 they moved to Waynesville, DeWitt county, Illinois. In the spring of 1839 moved to the farm which his father gave him, two and one-fourth miles northeast of Waynesville, Ill. He managed the farm and ran a blacksmith shop. His home was the stopping place for the weary traveler. Although they had a large family there was always room for the stranger. He and his wife were zealous members of M. E. Church, and he was class leader for many years. In the spring of 1857 he moved back to Waynesville, where he worked at his trade until near his death. He died January 27, 1862. His widow and daughters, Alma and Eva, lived in Waynesville until she died September 28, 1870. They had twelve children: William J. Zebulon G., Elizabeth, Ira J., Mary, Miles Trotter, Alma, Alma J., John E., Albert, Evaline, Marcus.

William J. Cantrall.

W. J. Cantrall, son of John M., son of Zebulon, was born in Sangamon county, Illinois, September 24, 1834. He was married to Lora A. Hickox, at Waynesville, Ill., February 14, 1856. She was born May 24, 1837. He enlisted in Company C, 14th Regiment Missouri sharpshooters, and served creditably until his health failed. In 1867 he moved with his family to Emporia, Kan. Here in 1871 his family was broken by the death of his wife, February 14, and he became a wanderer in search of health. In 1879 he went to North Dakota. In 1884, March 20, he was married to Mary E. Gilbert, of Chicago. His wife died April 12, 1885. April 15, 1886, he was married to Mrs. Emma E. Clark, of Chicago. She was sister to his second wife. In March, 1895, he moved to Detroit, Minn. There he died April 17, 1896. Mr. Cantrall was the father of three children, all by his first wife. Frederick A., born February 9, 1857; Nellie V., born in 1865; died in infancy; Frances A., born May 26, 1861.

Frederick Augustus Cantrall   Mary E. Cantrall.

F. A. Cantrall, only son of William J., was born
Waynesville, Ill., February 9, 1857. When he was 10 years old
his parents moved to Emporia, Kan. There his mother died
in 1871. He went with his father to Denver, Colo., where
he entered the office of the Denver Times, and learned the
trade of a printer. He worked in Denver until 1883, when
he went east, being in connection with the Chicago Inter
Ocean for seven years. Was with the Butte (Mont.) Miner
two years, and then returned to Denver, Colo., and is now
connected with the Denver Evening Post. January 19, 1878,
he was married to Mary E. Teeter, of Washington, Iowa. She
was born March 21, 1858. Their children are: Lora E., born
May 20, 1879; David Teeter, born January 10, 1881; died Sep
tember 10, 1881; Eva Vista, born October 7, 1882; Frederick
Ormsby, born July 7, 1887.

Zebulon Daniel Cantrell.

Z. D. Cantrell, son of John M., son of Zebulon G., was born August 28, 1833, two and one-half miles west of Cantrall, Sangamon county, Illinois. In 1834 his parents moved to Waynesville, Ill. When six years old his parents moved to the farm near Waynesville, where he grew to manhood. When he was 21 years old he and his father traveled across the country from Waynesville, to Clinton, Ill., looking for a farm. They could have purchased the best land for $1.25 per acre. They decided that the prairies could never be cultivated and that only a small strip along the timber would ever be fit for habitation. December 13, 1855, he married Susan Foreman, and in 1858, moved on a farm near Elm Grove, four and one-half miles southeast of Waynesville, Ill., where he improved one of the best farms in the State. Mr. Cantrell was Justice of the Peace for 25 years, and held many other positions of trust. In the fall of 1890, his son, Elmer, moved on the farm and he moved to Clinton, Ill. Here he lived until his death, May 16, 1897. Their children are: Carmi G., Joanna J., Elmer E., Thomas D., M. Angie.

Susan Cantrell.   Joanna J. Lanterman.

Susan Foreman, wife of Z. D. Cantrell was born March 21, 1835, near Pharisburg, Ohio. Her parents were Thomas and Mississippi Foreman. Her mother was born in what was known as the French settlement in Illinois, September 3, 1803. She was married to Z. D. Cantrell December 13, 1855. In 1858 Mr. and Mrs. Cantrell moved on a farm they bought of the Illinois Central Railroad Company, six miles west of Wapella, Ill. Their friends repeatedly said they would starve living so far from the timber. It would be impossible to describe their early experiences on the wild prairie. There was always room in their home for the traveler, and there seemed to be no limit when it came to entertaining friends. She and her granddaughter, Nina Lanterman, live in Clinton, Ill.

Joanna J. Cantrell, daughter of Z. D., was born June 13, 1859. She got her education in the public schools at Elm Grove, Ill., and in college at Lincoln, Ill. June 12, 1878, she was married to D. W. Lanterman. March 31, 1880, their only child, Nina Wenona, was born. Mrs. Cantrell died February 27, 1882. She is especially remembered for her efficiency in playing the organ and leading church music.

Carmi G. Cantrell.

C. G. Cantrell, eldest son of Z. D. Cantrell, was born in Waynesville Township, DeWitt county, Illinois, April 19, 1857. In 1858, his father moved on a farm in Barnett Township, DeWitt county, where he grew to manhood. His parents were faithful in having him attend the public school every winter until the fall of 1873, when he entered Illinois Wesleyan College, at Bloomington, Ill. He remained there two years. Then he returned to the farm. January 1, 1879, he was married to Mary O. Bell, of Richwood, Ohio. They moved on a farm in Barnett Township, DeWitt county, Illinois, where they lived until the fall of 1889, when they moved to Eureka, Ill., where Mr. Cantrell entered college again, preparatory to entering the Christian ministry, which he did while yet in school. He just closed a three and one-half years' pastorate at Williamsville, Ill., and has moved to Irvington, Ind. Mr. Cantrell is a member of the Masons, I. O. O. F. and K. of P.; also of the M. W. of A.

15

Mary Orline Cantrell.

Mary O. Bell, daughter of Enos A. and Naomi Bell, was
born near Pharisburgh, Ohio, June 4, 1860. January 1, 1879,
she was married to C. G. Cantrell, of Waynesville, Ill. Both
having been raised on a farm, they came to Illinois and lived
on a farm in DeWitt county until September, 1889, when they
moved to Eureka, Ill., where Mr. Cantrell entered college.
After living there two years they moved to Table Grove, Ill.
August, 1898, they moved to Irvington, Ind. Their children
are: Dora Imo, born December 19, 1880; Anna May, born
September 27, 1882; Guy Leslie, born October 18, 1885; Ada
Luella, born November 16, 1891; died May 28, 1893; Carmi
Miles, born November 1, 1894.

Elmer E. Cantrell.   Jennie E. Cantrell.

E. E. Cantrell was born on the farm in DeWitt county, Illinois, August 21, 1861, where he grew to manhood. Farming during the summer, attended school in the winter. December 24, 1884, he married Jennie E. Britten. She was born April 27, 1861. Her parents died when she was young. She was making her home with her Uncle John Britten, when she was married. Mr. Cantrell chose for his lifework that of farming, and is one of the best farmers in that part of the country. In the fall of 1890 he moved on the old home place; his father moved to Clinton, Ill. Since his father's death he has owned the home farm, which is one of the best farms in that part of the country. They have five children: Raper Z., born November 14, 1885; Floyd S., born November 26, 1887; Alma F., born June 23, 1890; Mary Abbie, born February 24, 1892; Jennie Lelah, born April 12, 1896. Mr. Cantrell belongs to the Modern Woodmen of America, and is an enthusiastic member of the Masonic Order.

Thomas D. Cantrell, M. D.

Dr. Thomas D. Cantrell, youngest son of Z. D. Cantrell, was born on the farm, in Barnett Township, DeWitt county, Illinois, February 3, 1864, where he grew to manhood. Farming during the summer and attending school each winter unt'l the fall of 1884, he entered the Wesleyan University at Bloomington, Illinois, attending one year. In 1885 he then entered Rush Medical College, at Chicago, taking a full three years' course, graduating with honors February 21, 1888. August 31, 1887, he was married to Miss Marietta Arnett, of McLean county, Illinois, spending their first winter in Chicago. After practicing for three years in McLean and Ford counties, they moved to Clinton, Illinois, where he still practices his chosen profession. Their children are: Leta Fern, born February 21, 1889; Leona Fay, born November 6, 1890; died December 4, 1890.

James P. Lichtenberger.

James P. Lichtenberger was born near Decatur, Ill., June 10, 1870. His boyhood was spent on the farm. At the age of 17 he entered Eureka College, graduating with the class of '93. While a senior in college he was married to M. Angeline Cantrell. After leaving college he entered the ministry of the Christian Church, and has held pastorates at Greenview, Paxton and Canton. Their present home is at Canton, where Mr. Lichtenberger is pastor of one of the leading churches of the State. He has also won a reputation as an evangelist.

M. Angeline Lichtenberger.

M. Angeline Cantrell, youngest child of Z. D. Cantrell was born on the old home farm in DeWitt county, Illinois, January 10, 1872. She is a graduate of Clinton High School. She spent one year in teaching and one year in Eureka College, where she met and on June 29, 1892, married J. P. Lichtenberger of the class of '93. On March 25, while living in Eureka, a little daughter, Muriel, was born. She is now a bright little maid of five summers, and in Canton, on March 19, their second daughter, Yolande, was born. Mrs. Lichtenberger is a blonde and a perfect specimen of the Cantrell type.

Ira J. Cantrall.

I. J. Cantrell was born April 23, 1837, in Waynesville, Ill. Grew up on his father's farm. At the age of 18 went to Bloomington and learned the blacksmith trade. Went to Kansas Territory in the spring of 1858, and engaged in helping off the army to the Utah war. Went to Pike's Peak in 1859, returned to Illinois that fall and was married to Miss Martha Wooton December 15, 1859, who died September 23, 1860. March, 1863, emigrated to California. Lived in Stockton one year, went from there to the Idaho gold fields. Remained there one and one-half years and from there returned to the land of his birth, Illinois, and engaged in manufacturing carriages and wagons in Lincoln, Ill., until 1880. He celebrated his second marriage to Miss Sarah J. McLaughlin August 23, 1866, near Lincoln, Ill. She was born April 14, 1838. From this union six children were born. In 1880 he moved with his family to Fredonia, Kan., and from their to Kansas City, Mo., in 1888. Their children are: Gilbert H., Myra M., Ira J., Cyrus D., Luella and Estella.

Gilbert Harwood Cantrell.   Ira J. Cantrell, Jr.   Cyrus Duncan Cantrell.

G. H. Cantrell was born April 12, 1869. Lived with his parents until 18 years of age. Engaged in the mercantile business in Kansas City, Mo., and has chosen that for his lifework. He has been a traveling salesman for several years in the packing house products. Is now with the Dold Packing Co., of Kansas City, Mo. Was married to Miss Ethel Nichol, Kansas City, Mo., September 30, 1896. She was born November 1, 1875.

Ira J., Jr., and Cyrus Duncan Cantrell (twins) born in Lincoln, Ill., August 18, 1873. Attended the public schools until they graduated in 1888. Ira J. chose the profession of bookkeeper and has been with the Kansas & Texas Coal Company for several years, and is now cashier at McAlester, Indian Territory. Cyrus is engaged in working his way up to an M. D. The only men twins ever heard of in the Cantrell tribe, hale and hearty, stout young men.

Elizabeth Shirley.   Mary Harper.

Elizabeth Cantrell, daughter of John M., son of Zebulon
G., was born May 9, 1835, near Waynesville, Ill. September
21, 1855, she was married to Robert King. They lived on a
farm near Waynesville, Ill., until Mr. King's death, July 9,
1858, when she moved to Waynesville with her children, Alice
M., Charlie, Hattie B., where they lived eight years. March
13, 1866, she married William P. Shirley. They moved to a
farm near Leroy, Ill. They had two children, Nellie and
Grace. Mr. Shirley died September 10, 1883. Mrs. Shirley
moved to Leroy, Ill., where she now lives.

Mary Cantrell, daughter of John M., was born near
Waynesville, Ill., July 13, 1840. Dec. 17, 1863, she was mar-
ried to Milam Harper, at Waynesville, Ill. They moved to
Kansas, where she died October 30, 1875. Their children are:
Edwin and Nettie are dead. Harriet and Joanna (twins),
born November 18, 1869, are married and have families. Har-
riet married Arthur L. Tucker. They live near Harper, Kan.
Joanna married Martin L. Gates. They live near Anthony,
Kan.

Miles Trotter Cantrell.

M. T. Cantrell was born November 11, 1843, on a farm near Waynesville, Ill. He received a common school education and began teaching in 1861, and taught 11 years. He was a soldier in Company E, 68th Illinois Volunteer Infantry, serving most of the time in the army of the Potomac. December 24, 1863, he married Isabelle Achers Martin, in Atlanta, Ill. Their children are: Corwin C., Ingham, Ann Maria, John N., Samuel T., Vida L., Harry G., James T. Mr. Cantrell moved to Kansas in 1872, farmed for eight years, then was appointed Deputy Postmaster at Fredonia, Kan. He had entire charge over the office for five years when he was appointed Postmaster, and served until change of administration. For eight years was engaged in the hardware implement business. Then for some years engaged in the creamery and milling business. He now has charge of the postoffice at Fredonia, Kan., as deputy, with a four-year contract. Mr. Cantrell is a member of the Presbyterian Church and is an active worker. Four of their children died young. Corwin C. is married and lives at Fredonia, Kan. Samuel T. is in the 'Frisco General Freight Office at Wichita, Kan.

Alma J. Gring.   Evaline Harrold.

Alma J. Cantrell was the daughter of John M., son of Zebulon G.; was born November 5, 1847. After her father's death she lived with her mother in Waynesville, Ill., and taught school. After her mother's death she made her home with her sister, Elizabeth. She taught school altogether for fifteen years, and November 23, 1880, married John W. Gring. They have two children, Harry C., born July 3, 1882; Estella, born September 12, 1887.

Evaline Cantrell was born November 16, 1853, near Waynesville, Ill. When she was nine years old her father died and she and her sister, Alma, lived with their mother. When she was 17 years old her mother died, after which she attended school in Lincoln, Ill., living with her brother, Ira. Then she went to her sister, Mary, in Kansas; there she taught school for a time, then returned to Illinois, making her home with her brother, Zebulon, teaching school. October 19, 1876, she was married to W. S. Harrold. June 12, 1885, she died, leaving four children. Roy M., born April 11, 1878; Berzie A., born November 27, 1879; John L., born February 17, 1881; died September 6, 1882; Laura B., born June 26, 1882. Mr. Harrold is married again and lives on a farm, two and one-half miles west of Wapella, Ill.

John Edward Cantrell   Fred Ball.

J. E. Cantrell, son of John M., son of Zebulon G., was born on a farm November 9, 1849. When he was 16 years of age he went to Lincoln, Ill., and learned the wagonmaker's trade. From there he went to Champaign University, where he became one of the leading mechanics. From over work and exposure he took sick and was compelled to give up his school work, went to his brother Zebulon's, and from there to his brother Ira's, in Lincoln, Ill., where, after four months of sickness, he died May 2, 1872.

Fred Ball was born in Logan county, Illinois, November 17, 1862, where he lived until 1885, when he went to Iowa, and during that year came to DeWitt county, locating at Waynesville. In June, 1892, he graduated from the Wesleyan Law School. October 9, 1893, he was married to Ivanilla Dunham, of Waynesville, Ill. She is daughter of W. W. Dunham, whose mother was Eliza Cantrell, wife of Jeremiah P. Dunham, daughter of Zebulon G. Cantrell. They have one child, Frederick, born March 23, 1895. Mr. Ball is one of the leading attorneys of DeWitt county, Ill.

James Madison Cantrell.   Eliza Cantrell.

James M. Cantrell, son of Zebulon G., was born April 10, 1810, in Kentucky. When he was a small child his parents moved to Clark county, Ohio. Grew to manhood there, and was married to Eliza McLaughlin August 9, 1832. That fall they moved to Illinois, settling on a farm near Waynesville. During the remaining years of his life, he remained very near the place where he first settled. He died April 27, 1866. His wife was born in Ohio, March 22, 1811, and died June 14, 1881. To them were born three daughters: Sarah J., born July 13, 1833; died January 21, 1857; Elmira A., born January 11, 1837; Eliza J. W., born August 30, 1847.

Zebulon Pike Cantrell.   Sarah A. Funk.

Z. P. Cantrell, son of Zebulon G., was born January 17, 1814, in Springfield, Ohio. In 1833 moved to Illinois, with his parents. He was a shoemaker by trade and was also a plasterer. He married Elizabeth Paulk October 16, 1838. She was born January 11, 1818. They had six children: Amos A., William L., Martha J., Sarah A., Mary E., Eliza D.

His wife died June 12, 1852, and he married Rachel Doyle November 16, 1852. They had two children, William Doyle and Edgar L. His second wife died in the fall of 1865, and he married Mrs. Mary Harp, whose maiden name was Everly, March 14, 1872. He died April 24, 1876, near Chestnut, Ill. His widow lived with her brother-in-law, William L. Cantrell until her death, January 5, 1895.

Sarah A. Cantrell, daughter of Zebulon Pike, was born December 25, 1844. Her mother died when she was eight years old. March 23, 1871, she was married to Theodore A. Funk. One child was born to them, and he died in infancy. Mrs. Funk died April 30, 1872, near Cerro Gordo, Ill. Mr. Funk lives in Decatur, Ill.

Amos A. Cantrell.

A. A. Cantrell, son of Zebulon P., son of Zebulon G., was was born May 11, 1840, near Waynesville, Ill., and lived on the farm until he enlisted September 20, 1861, in Company L, Fourth Illinois Cavalry, and was honorably discharged from Company I, 12th Illinois Cavalry, June 18, 1866. During the service he was much in battle—Fort Henry, Fort Donelson and at Battle of Coffeeville, Miss. He was home after the Battle of Fort Donelson for sixty days, except that, he was never off duty and was never wounded. Mr. Cantrell belongs to the G. A. R. Harvey H. Merriman was his Captain. Mr. Cantrell was Corporal and re-enlisted February 28, 1864, as veteran volunteer; was sergeant of Man's Company I, 12th Regiment Illinois Cavalry. He is a member of the G. A. R., of Areli Lodge, I. O. O. F., No. 599, Cisco, Ill., Fraternal Encampment 145, Monticello, Ill., Bethel Rebekah Degree Lodge No. 253, Monticello, Ill. Mr. Cantrell was never married, and for the past thirty years has lived at Cisco, Ill.

Samuel G. Mott.　　　　　　Martha Jane Mott.

S. G. Mott was born in Ohio June 28, 1832. In the spring of 1862 he moved to Illinois, where he has since lived. June 19, 1862, he married Martha J. Cantrell, daughter of Zebulon Pike, son of Zebulon G., at Newburgh, Ill. She was born October 3, 1842, near Waynesville, Ill. Her mother died when she was but 10 years of age. For a time she made her home with her Uncle John M. Cantrell, afterward kept house for her father. Since her marriage they have lived on a farm. Their children are: George A., born March 14, 1863; Sarah E., born November 8, 1864; Lewis A., born February 4, 1867; James A., born January 11, 1869; Clarissa E., born February 24, 1872; Joseph A., born September 10, 1873; Lillie E., born December 3, 1875; Alonzo A., born January 3, 1877; Theodora A., born March 21, 1880; Clarence, born August 10, 1884. Their home now is four miles southeast of Blue Mound, Ill.

Edmund C. Hunsley.   Mary E. Hunsley.

E. C. Hunsley was born in England, September 12, 1841.
He was a school teacher by profession. Came to America,
and January 12, 1871, married Mary E. Cantrell, daughter of
Zebulon Pike, son of Zebulon G. She was born in Logan
county, Ill., Jan. 8, 1848. When 13 years old her mother died
and she kept house for her father. Her husband enlisted Aug.
15, 1862, in Company G, 10th Regiment Illinois Cavalry. His
captain was Wm. T. Wooten. He was honorably discharged
June 5, 1865. After the war he kept a book store for two years
in Bement, Ill., then moved to a farm near Cisco, Ill., where
they lived until a short time ago, when they moved to Cisco,
Ill., where they now live. Mrs. Hunsley is an enthusiastic
W. C. T. U. worker. Their children are: Laura Agnes, born
November 1, 1871; Inis Arabella, born December 27, 1872; died
September 26, 1873; John Irving, born June 30, 1874; George
Howard, born April 1, 1876; Mahlon Arthur, born May 22,
1878; Charles Pike, born October 20, 1880; Mary Emily, born
September 6, 1882; Frank, born March 14, 1885; died Novem-
ber 2, 1886; Marcellas Edmond, born July 11, 1891.

Jeremiah Perry Dunham.

Eliza Cantrall, daughter of Zebulon G., was born July 1, 1816, in Ohio. Came to Illinois with her parents in 1831. October 5, 1834 she married J. P. Dunham, at Williamsville. He was born in Providence, R. I., March 3, 1811. Died January 9, 1897. When he was about one year old his parents moved to Ohio. They came to Illinois in the spring of 1831. Began his married life three miles west of Waynesville, where he farmed in the summer and taught school in the winter. He served as Justice of the Peace for 13 years, and was Probate Judge of Logan county for three years. In 1851 moved to Waynesville, where he become a merchant. Was very successful in that business and continued until his death. They had seven children: Mary Lauressa, Helen A., Amy Letitia, William W., Rebecca Snow, Eliza, Jeremiah P. J. P. Dunham, Jr., is the only one that I have learned of that died with cholera.

Rachel Graves.

Rachel Cantrell, daughter of Zebulon G., was born April 25, 1818. She was married to Charles Graves October 8, 1840, at Waynesville, Ill. He was born in Vermont, April 30, 1817. Five children were born to them, three of whom died in infancy; the other two, Fannie S., born September 11, 1841; John W., born July 19, 1850. Mr. Graves moved from place to place until finally in April, 1850, he left his family in Illinois and started for California, and never has been heard from. It is supposed that he died in crossing the plains. Mrs. Graves raised her children, and after they were married made her home with them, staying most of the time with her daughter. She died at her son's, in Decatur, Ill., March 25, 1892, and was buried beside her twin sister, Rebecca Sampson, at Waynesville, Ill. Her sister died March 25, 1849.

John William Graves.

John W. Graves, son of Rachel, daughter of Zebulon G. Cantrell, was born July 19, 1850, on a farm near Waynesville, Ill. February 22, 1865, he enlisted when only 14 years old in Wisconsin, in Company K, 46th Wisconsin Volunteer Infantry, and served until the close of the war. He then returned to Wisconsin and lived on a farm for nine years, then went to Winona, Wisconsin, and became a fireman on the Chicago and Northwestern Railroad, afterwards moving to Centralia, Ill., and worked for Illinois Central Railroad for four years. March 8, 1877, he married Martha Jane Edds. She was born June 29, 1848. He has since lived in Decatur, Ill. Mr. Graves is a member of Macon Lodge No. 8, A. F. and A. M., the first Lodge chartered by the Grand Lodge of Illinois. It was chartered October 5, 1841. He is also a member of Macon Chapter No. 21, organized September 29, 1854. Bean Manoir No. 9, K. T. He is also a member of Goodman Band, one of the best in the State; also belongs to G. A. R. He is a carpenter and works in the Union Iron works, Decatur, Ill. Their children, Edna C., born February 8, 1878; Vella A., born September 5, 1880; died September 27, 1882; Mattie A., born January 9, 1883; Walter A., born August 10, 1885; Nina Hazel, born January 26, 1888.

William L. Cantrell.

William L. Cantrell, youngest son of Zebulon G. Cantrell, was born May 15, 1823, in Ohio. When he was 10 years old his father moved to Sangamon county, Illinois. In 1834 they moved to DeWitt county, Illinois. Mr. Cantrell was raised on a farm. October 26, 1843, he married Melinda Stout, at Clinton, Ill. At one time he owned and run the Tunbridge Mill. Most of his life was spent farming in Logan and De Witt counties. A few years before his death he lived in Ken ney, Ill. He was an enthusiastic member of the M. E. Church and was an earnest Sunday School worker, and for many years he was a class leader. He died June 28, 1895. They had eight children. Ann, born September 19, 1845; Emeline, born October 14, 1848; John K., born May 25, 1851; Lydia A., born October 14, 1853; died in infancy; Jessie, born June 2, 1856; William, born September 12, 1858; Sarah E. (Dora), born July 16, 1861; died July 1, 1864.

William Cantrell.   Effie Cantrell.

William Cantrell, son of William L., son of Zebulon G., was born September 12, 1858, near Kenney, Ill. Except nine months that they lived in Kansas, William has lived near his birthplace. June 12, 1879, he was married to Effie Kirby. She was born October 22, 1860. Her grand parents were among the earliest settlers of that part of the country. Her father is one of the leading farmers in that section. Mr. Cantrell is a farmer and stock raiser, and lives now one and one-half miles north of Kenney, Ill. They have three children: Wade Elmer, born January 10, 1881; Olive Gertrude, born June 21, 1883; Harry K., born April 16, 1889.

Irvin Johnson Danels.   Sarah Danels.

I. J. Danels, husband of Sarah Cantrell, daughter of
Joshua, son of Zebulon G., was born August 11, 1825, in
Ohio. His father died when he was three years old. He
came to Illinois April 6, 1845, to his Uncle Elijah Hull, one
mile south of Waynesville. In 1846 he commenced to learn
the wagonmaker's trade with Junius Sampson, in Waynesville. In 1847 he went to Pekin, Ill., and finished learning
his trade. He came back to Waynesville, where he married
Sarah Cantrell, February 17, 1848. She was born in Middle-
town, Ohio, and came to Sangamon county, Illinois, October
23, 1833, and in 1834, to Waynesville, Illinois. They lived in
Waynesville 18 years, then moved to a farm six and one-fourth
miles southeast of Waynesville, in 1867. There Mr. Danels
died May 19, 1898. Their children are: William, John, Edward, Anna, Jane P., Eliza A., Ida, Lida Ann, M. Cara. Ida
and her mother live at the home place. Joshua Cantrell died
October 27, 1860. His widow lives with her son, John S., in
Derby, Kan. She is in her 94th year, the oldest one of the
name.

John Humphrey.   Thirza Humphrey.

Thirza Cantrell, daughter of Joshua, was born December 25, 1802. Married John Humphrey January 8, 1825. He was born June 15, 1797. They came to Illinois in an early day and improved a farm near where Hallsville now is. By hard work and careful management they gathered about them considerable property. They were the parents of nine children. William F., born November 15, 1824; Joshua C., born November 26, 1826; Thomas C., born November 22, 1828; Zebulon R., born August 24, 1829; Milton, born November 8, 1832; Mary J., born November 17, 1834; Levi A., born July 18, 1837; Elizabeth E., born May 14, 1840; Rachel Annie, born January 19, 1844. Most of their children married and raised families, but they lived to see them all buried except Zebulon R. He died January 16, 1895. John Humphrey died November 17, 1882, and his wife died December 27, 1886.

Zebulon Cantrall.   Mary (Polly) Cantrall.

Zebulon Cantrall, son of Joshua, was born August 24, 1805, in Kentucky. In 1811, moved with his parents, to Clark county, Ohio. Married Mary McLain, March 27, 1828. She was born February 19, 1809. Died near Waynesville, February 22, 1882. Moved near Waynesville, Ill., in 1834, where he lived until his death, September 3, 1861. He and his wife were charter members of the Presbyterian Church at Waynesville, which was organized June 26, 1836. He was elected elder at the organization, which position he held until his death. He was a tanner by trade; also followed farming. For many years was Associate Judge of Logan county. Their children were: James McLain, born March 14, 1830; died November 28, 1868; Rachel McCollam, born August 8, 1834; died August 10, 1860. Robert Andrew, born October 23, 1836; died September 13, 1845. Smith Minturn, born August 28, 1839. Thomas Dunham, born March 27, 1841. Mary Elizabeth, born June 30, 1845; died March 1, 1848. Charles Rogers, born June 9, 1853.

Thomas Dunham Cantrall.   H. Alma Cantrall.

Thomas D. Cantrall, son of Zebulon, son of Joshua, was born March 27, 1841, near Waynesville, Ill. September 22, 1863, married H. Alma Fox, of Madison county, Ohio. They lived on their farm adjoining the old homestead near Waynesville, Ill., until 1876, when they moved to Fredonia, Kansas, where they engaged in farming. Mr. Cantrall united with the Presbyterian Church at Waynesville, Ill., when about 15 years of age. At the organization of the First Presbyterian Church, of Fredonia, Kansas, he was elected deacon. Their children are: Frank Ross, born November 30, 1865; Charles McKee, born August 1, 1869; Robert Fox, born January 28, 1874; Jessie McLain, born September 23, 1877. Their son, Charles McKee, is a minister in the Presbyterian Church. Their home now is near Fredonia, Kan.

Charles McKee Cantrall.   Anna Hawley Cantrall.

C. M. Cantrall, son of Thomas D., son of Zebulon, son of Joshua, was born August 1, 1869, near Waynesville, Ill. Married Anna Hawley Wood, at Fredonia, Kan., June 28, 1893. She was born in Marysville, Ohio, October 25, 1870, united with the Presbyterian Church, of Fredonia, Kan., in 1889. Daughter of Harvey S. Wood, First Lieutenant Company F, 16th Ohio Volunteers, and Sarah Philips, of Richmond, Ohio. Mr. Cantrall graduated from Fredonia High School in May, 1891. Attended college at Emporia, Kansas, and Center College, Danville, Kentucky. Graduated from the Presbyterian Theological Seminary at Danville, Kentucky, May 5, 1898. Served as missionary of Presbyterian Board of Publication and Sunday School Work, Synod of Nebraska, from October 1, 1892, to November 1, 1894. Stated supply of Presbyterian churches of Weir City, Cherokee, Kansas, from November 10, 1894, until September 10, 1895, when he entered the Seminary and served the church of Moran, Kan., as stated supply with view to pastorate. Licensed by Neosha Presbyterian Synod in Kansas, April 5, 1898. Their children are: Thomas Harvey, born August 20, 1894; died September 13, 1894. Archibald Martin, born August 30, 1896, in Danville, Kentucky.

Sherman Grant Hull.

S. G. Hull, son of Joshua, son of Mahala, daughter of Joshua Cantrall, was born March 6, 1867, on a farm three miles west of Wapella, Ill. In 1889 entered the Northwestern School of Pharmacy. In 1893 completed the course of pharmacy in Chicago. In that year engaged in the drug business in Clinton, Ill. March 8, 1894, married Leona May Harrison, in Clinton, Ill. They have one child, Cecil B., born February 28, 1895. Mr. Hull is a member of the Modern Woodmen of America; also a member of the Plantangenet No. 25, K. P.; also of the Uniform Rank, K. P. He is a member of Olive Lodge No. 98, I. O. O. F., Clinton, Ill. Mr. Hull's store is on the west side of the square, Clinton, Ill. His father enlisted in Captain Evans Richards' Company E, of the 20th Regiment, Illinois Volunteer Infantry, serving until September 1, 1862, when he was severely wounded through the right lung and right forearm and was discharged November 16, 1862.

William Cantrall.　　　　　　　　Nancy Cantrall.

W. Cantrall was born April 1, 1812, in Ohio. Grew to manhood on the farm. November 27, 1834, married Nancy McClure. She was born July 27, 1810. In 1844 they moved to Waynesville, Ill. He run the old mill for a time. Settled up the business for Ormsby and Scherr, one of the largest firms in that day. He and his brother-in-law, William Jones, run the first brick yard in that country. He and his wife were members of the Presbyterian Church. Their children, Henry M., Rachel P., Margaret and William H. Henry and Margaret died in infancy. Rachel P. was born December 5, 1838. Married William Metzger, and lives in Clinton, Ill. William H. was born December 27, 1843. Married Deborah Earson and lives on a farm one mile south of Waynesville, Ill. William Cantrall died December 15, 1886. His wife died September 13, 1874.

Levi Cantrall.   Elizabeth G. Cantrall.

Levi Cantrall, son of Joshua, was born May 6, 1814, in Ohio. In his seventeenth year he united with the Presbyterian Church. In the fall of 1835 the family moved to a farm near Waynesville, Ill. October 17, 1839, he married Elizabeth G. Robb. She was born December 11, 1815. Their children are: L. Jennie, born October 27, 1840; died April 15, 1896. John R., born January 21, 1842. Nancy A., born April 29, 1844; died March 15, 1875. December 1, 1844, Mr. Cantrall was chosen as elder in the room of his father, who died August 11, 1840. He has been a member of the Presbyterian Church for more than 67 years. An active ruling elder for nearly 57 years, during which time he has not been absent from any communion service, nor from more than one stated meeting of the session. Mr. Cantrall's record in church work is probably the best of any man in the United States.

John R. Cantrall.   Alva L. Cantrall.

J. R. Cantrall, only son of Levi, son of Joshua, was born January 21, 1842. He grew to manhood on his father's farm at Waynesville. He enlisted in Company D, 107th Illinois Volunteers, August 6, 1862, and served three years and was mustered out at close of the war with regiment and returned home and took a course in commercial school in Chicago, 1865-66. He married Jennie Love October 6, 1870, at Waynesville, Ill. They moved to a farm near Hammond, Ill. In 1873 moved to Bloomington, Ill., where he engaged in the real estate business. In 1876 returned to the farm where they lived until 1889. They then moved to Tuscola, Ill., where he and his son are engaged in real estate, loan and insurance business. Their children are: Alva L., born August 2, 1871; Edna E., born March 11, 1873; Mertie M., born December 12, 1879; died November 8, 1897.

A. L. Cantrall, son of John R., was born August 2, 1871. Graduated from High School in Tuscola in 1892. In 1897 went in to partnership with his father in the real estate, loan and insurance business. His sister, Mertie Maud, died when 18 years old. His sister, Edna E., graduated from High School in 1893, then took a course in training school for nurses in St. Louis, Mo., graduating in 1896. Since then has been private nurse in St. Louis, Mo.

Nancy Robb.   Joshua C. Robb.

N. Cantrall, daughter of Joshua, was born June 13, 1816, in Ohio. Moved to Illinois. Married James R. Robb March 26, 1840. He was born July 26, 1814. They lived on a farm two miles east of Waynesville, Ill., where her husband died November 16, 1847, leaving three children, Joshua C., born March 21, 1841; Francis Marion, born November 19, 1842; Hugh, born September 3, 1846. After her husband's death, Mrs. Robb moved to the home of her brother, Joshua Cantrall, where they lived four years, then moved to Waynesville, where they lived with her brother, Eli Cantrall, for three years, then moved back to the farm in the spring of 1855. She and her boys managed the farm. The two older boys enlisted in the army. Joshua died one year after he enlisted. Marion returned to the farm after the war. She and her son, Hugh, moved to Heyworth, Ill., in 1871, where she died December 15, 1894.

J. C. Robb, son of Nancy, daughter of Joshua Cantrall, was born March 21, 1841, on a farm two miles east of Waynesville, Ill. April 22, 1861, he enlisted in Company E, 20th Illinois Infantry, for three months, then re-enlisted, but his health failed and he returned home and died April 28, 1862, after six weeks of sickness.

16

Francis Marion Robb.   Hugh Robb.

F. M. Robb, son of Nancy, daughter of Joshua Cantrall, was born November 19, 1842, on the farm two miles east of Waynesville, Ill. He enlisted July, 1862, for three years in Company D, 107th Illinois Infantry. He was in convalescent camp at Knoxville, Tenn., for about six months, was in the siege of Vicksburg. After the war he moved to Hillsboro, Ill., where he farmed and run his saw mill. He died there March 9, 1886. Married Alvira Bridges, September 27, 1866. She was born August 20, 1848. They had one daughter, Maud A., born July 12, 1867. She married E. H. McFarland, September 7, 1892.

H. Robb, son of Nancy, daughter of Joshua Cantrall, was born September 3, 1846, on a farm two miles east Waynesville, Ill., where he lived most of the time until 1871, when he moved to Heyworth, Ill., where he worked in a grocery store for a time, then in a drug store, where he now is. For a number of years has owned and managed a drug store. February 26, 1880, he married Josie S. Scroggy. She was born at Thorntown, Indiana, November 29, 1853. Mr. Robb has been a member of the Presbyterian Church for more than 30 years, and is now one of the trustees. He is also a member of Heyworth Lodge No. 183, I. O. O. F., and Aetna Lodge No. 412, K. P.

Joshua C Cantrall.

J. C. Cantrall, son of Joshua, was born in Clark county, Ohio, September 20, 1818. When 17 years old he came with his parents to Waynesville, DeWitt county, Ill. He lived on the farm south of town, where the family first settled, where his father and mother lived and died, till the year 1875, when he moved to Waynesville, where he lived until his death, March 31, 1897. He united with the Presbyterian Church in 1840; was an active member, serving many years as one of the elders. He was superintendent of the Sunday School for 35 years, 27 years without intermission. April 29, 1841, he married Mary Jane Robb. She was born May 30, 1823. Their children are: Nancy Jane, Martha Ann, and a son, these died in infancy. The living children are: James, born June 19, 1845, and lives south of Waynesville on the home farm. Rachel, born December 13, 1850. Married Alva C. Ingham. Lives near Warrensburg, Macon county, Ill.

James Cantrall.

James Cantrall, son of Joshua C. Cantrall, son of Joshua, was born June 19, 1845, near Waynesville, Ill., on the farm where his grandfather settled in 1835. There he grew to manhood. November 24, 1870, he was married to Mary J. Lanham. She was born January 10, 1843. They moved from Waynesville, Ill., to Decatur, where they lived for a time, then returned to Waynesville, to the old home farm. Their children are: Farrel, born January 16, 1872; died October 7, 1872. Earnest, born July 16, 1874; died September 28, 1874. Nellie M., born August 8, 1875. Mabel C., born March 12, 1879. Mrs. Cantrall, died March 30, 1889, and Mr. Cantrall married Mrs. Christina H. Stewart, whose maiden name was Huckleberry, November 28, 1889. They moved to Indiana, where they lived for a time, and now live on the old farm again near Waynesville, Ill., this being their home since the death of Mr. Cantrall's father, March 31, 1897. Mr. Cantrall is a carpenter and has built him a comfortable house on the old farm. He is a member of the M. E. Church, and is an active worker in the same.

Polly Jones.

Polly Jones, daughter of Joshua Cantrall, was born February 8, 1810, in Kentucky. Moved to Ohio, then to Illinois. May 21, 1839, she was married to William H. Jones. This was the first wedding in the county, in DeWitt county, after it was organized. He was born January 18, 1812, in Kentucky. Mr. Jones was a brick mason and also a carpenter. He made the brick and built a number of brick houses in the vicinity of Waynesville, Ill. He improved a farm one mile east of where Hallsville, Ill., now is, and lived there until his death, February 3, 1872. His wife died May 10, 1872. They had seven children, Hester Ann, born September 16, 1840; Lucinda Moore, born January 15, 1842; James T., born October 28, 1843; Rachel E., born September 29, 1845; Nancy J., born December 20, 1846; William H., born May 24, 1848; Mary E., born July 21, 1853.

William Graham Cantrall.

W. G. Cantrall, the sixth son of Joshua, was born September 6, 1784, in Virginia. His parents moved to Kentucky in 1789. There he married Deborah Mitts. She was born in Virginia, November 16, 1785. Soon after marriage they moved to Ohio, then moved to Sangamon County, where they lived until the death of Mrs. Cantrall, March 15, 1856. He then made his home with his son, Joshua M., until he died, March 6, 1867. He was a faithful member of the Christian Church, and for many years one of the deacons. He was Justice of the Peace for over twenty years, being elected in 1821 for the first time. He was the father of twelve children. Dorothy, Ann, Eliabeth, Joshua M., Thirza, Adam M., Deborah, Mahala, Susannah, William M., Miranda and Andrew Jackson.

Andrew J. died when 13 years old. The rest all lived to raise families except Mahalah, who was married three times but raised no children. Miranda is the only one living. She married Samuel Mellinger.

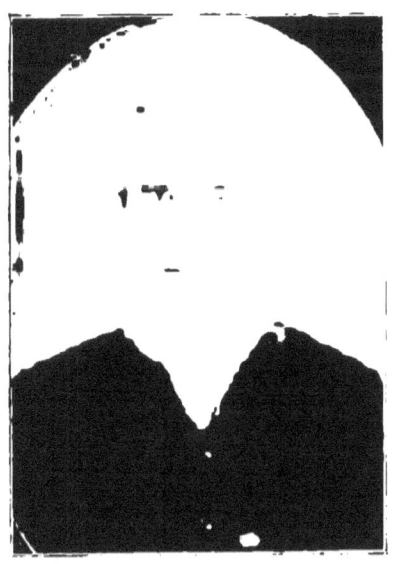

Joshua Mitts Cantrall.   Sarah Cantrall.

J. M. Cantrall, son of William G., was born Dec. 17, 1810, in Ohio. His entire life was spent on the farm. In 1824 he came with his parents to Illinois. They settled two miles south of Cantrall, Ill., where he and his parents lived and died. January 14, 1834, he married Sarah Cantrell, daughter of Zebulon G. She was born March 14, 1812. He and his wife became members of the Christian Church at the same time. He was an active member of the Cantrall Church for more than 50 years, serving as one of its elders most of that time. There were ten children in their family. Zebulon G., William G., Matilda, Isaac, Jacob M., Joshua G., Mahala E., Sarah, John A., and George A. Four of their children lived to raise families. His wife died November 28, 1887. He made his home with his son, William G., until his death January 18, 1884.

Zebulon Graham Cantrall.　　　　　　Elizabeth Jane Cantrall.

Z. G. Cantrall, son of Joshua M., son of William G., was born May 7, 1835, in Sangamon County, Illinois, where he grew to manhood. November 6, 1864, he married Elizabeth J. Lilly. She was born November 19, 1838, near Stanton, Virginia. She, with her parents, moved to Illinois, in 1855. Mr. Cantrall lived on a farm fourteen years after marriage, near Cantrall, Ill. He was a carpenter by trade as well as a farmer. He was elected Assessor of Fancy Creek Township for seven years and was Collector for three years. They moved to Springfield, Ill., in 1880, where they lived two years, then moved back to the farm and stayed two years, when they returned to Springfield, where he lived until his death, May 3, 1896. Their children: Mary A., Melissa E., Celia J., Noah, Arminda L., Amelia F., twins, Alfred E., Zebulon G., Mary, Noah, Arminda and Amelia are dead. Malissa married William Womack and lives in Springfield, Ill. Celia J. married Frank A. Gillman, and lives in Indianapolis, Ind. Alfred and Zebulon live with their mother in Springfield, Ill.

William Graham Cantrall.   Mary Jane Cantrall

W. G. Cantrall, son of Joshua M., son of William G., was born February 20, 1837, near Cantrall, Ill. January 5, 1862, he married Mary Jane Randall, at Blue Mound, Ill. She was born January 26, 1839. She was daughter of Marshall S. Randall, who married Deborah Cantrall. Mr. Cantrall is a farmer and resides two and one-half miles south of Cntrall, Ill., near where his grandfather settled. They had nine children, Marcus Newton, Sarah Matilda, Mary Laurissa, Louisa Mahala, Deborah Anna, Rebecca Frances, John William, Ida Narcissus, Wilbur Franklin. Four of their children died young. Four of them married and have families. One, Wilbur Franklin, is at home.

Jacob M. Cantrall.   Marion J. Cantrall.

J. M. Cantrall, son of Joshua, son of William G., was born Dec. 26, 1841, two miles south of Cantrall, Ill., on a farm. There he grew to manhood. Dec. 22, 1869, he married Marion J. Tufts. She was born May 14, 1848, near Rochester, N. Y. Her parents came to Sangamon county in 1856. January 9, 1871, Sarah and Leucretia (twins) were born. They died in infancy. Addie E., born February 7, 1873. Married Edward Morgret. They live on a farm near Stonington, Ill. Cora M., born October 12, 1878. Married James M. Alexander and lives with her father. Mrs. Cantrall died March 26, 1879, and Mr. Cantrall married Martha Brown. January 15, 1880. She was born August 28, 1861. To them two sons were born, Jacob Earnest, born July 15, 1883; Ula Joshua, born June 1886. Mr. Cantrall is a farmer and lives on the farm where he was born. He joined the Christian Church on the First Lord's day, August, 1862, and has been an active member ever since. His wife was a member of the church for many years before her death. He is a member of the Home Forum at Cantrall, Ill. His second wife died January 16, 1898.

Martha Cantrall.   Lucy E. Mellinger.

Martha Brown was born August 28, 1861. Was married
to Jacob M. Cantrall January 15, 1880. Her parents, Peter
A. and Mary Brown, were among the early settlers of Menard
county. Moved to Sangamon county in 1871. Her father
died February 3, 1891. Her mother lives with her daughter,
Sarah Campbell. Martha Cantrall was the mother of two
boys, Jacob Earnest and Ula Joshua. Their mother died
January 16, 1898. The boys are at home with their father on
the farm. She was a faithful member of the Christian
Church, at Cantrall, Ill.; also a charter member of the Home
Forum Benefit Order, at Cantrall, Ill.

Lucy E. Mellinger, daughter of Samuel and Miranda Mellinger, was born November 11, 1866. Her mother is the only
child of William G. Cantrall. She lives with her parents on
the farm three miles south of Cantrall, Ill.

Marshall S. Randall.   Deborah Randall.

Deborah Cantrall, daughter of William G., was born February 16, 1817. Married Marshall S. Randall January 5, 1837. He was born January 26, 1813, in Kentucky. He came with his parents to Illinois in 1827. They were married in Sangamon county. Moved to a farm in Christian county, about 1853; moved near Blue Mound, where he and his wife died. His son, Isaac, lives on the old home place. They had twelve children, John W., Mary Jane, William H., Garrett D., Elizabeth, Louisa, Rachel, Nancy, Louis T., Deborah, Walter S., Isaac Newton. The children all married and raised families. Garrett T. is dead. Most of the others live near Blue Mound, Ill. Mr. Randall died September 15, 1883, and his widow June 10, 1891.

Samuel Mellinger,

Miranda Mellinger,

Miranda Cantrall, daughter of William G., was born May 12, 1826, in Sangamon county, Illinois. She was married to William C. Snelson, July 17, 1852. They had one child, Charles H., born April 17, 1853. Mr. Snelson died March 9, 1853, and his widow married Samuel Mellinger, March 4, 1858. He was born January 27, 1832, in Pennsylvania. Left there when 21 years old. In 1851 started west, stayed one year in Ohio, then came to Levi Cantrall's, near Cantrall, Ill. Except three years that he was in the army, he has lived in Sangamon county, never changing his voting place. Mr. Mellinger enlisted August 18, 1862, in Company C., 114th Illinois Infantry, serving three years, and was honorably discharged August 3, 1865. During the war he was in the battle of Jackson, Miss., at the siege and capture of Vicksburg, and the battle of Guntown. They have lived on the farm given his wife by her father, for the past forty years, which is three miles south of Cantrall, Ill.

Levi Cantrall.　　　　　　　　　　Ann Cantrall.

Levi Cantrall, son of Joshua Cantrall, was born October 1, 1787, in Virginia. His parens moved to Kentucky in 1789. He married Fannie England November 30, 1809. She was born October 2, 1792. He is company with his father-in-law, Stephen England, came to Illinois in 1819, and camped where Springfield now stands December 4. He was left an orphan when 12 years old and was bound to a man who was a tanner. He whipped him so severely that he carried the scars, showing them even in his old age to his friends. At the age of 14 he ran away from his master and made his own living. He was the father of eighteen children. He taught his children to show kindness to the poor and needy by relating to them his own hardships when young. His first wife died September 10, 1835, and he married Mrs. Ann Barnett, whose maiden name was Patterson, May 27, 1836. She was the mother of Fannie L. and Joseph S. Levi Cantrall died February 22, 1869, and his widow lived with her son, Joseph, until her death. The town of Cantrall, Ill., was laid out on land he entered soon after coming to the county and was named in honor of his memory.

Thomas Cantrall.   Thomas E. Cantrall.

Thomas Cantrall, son of Levi, was born October 11, 1810. He married Priscilla D. McLemore October 3, 1831. She was born September 11, 1814, in Tennessee. They had nine children: Clarissa, Turner H., Young M., Levi, Nancy A., Thomas J., Fannie P., Mary E., James D. His wife died, and he married Elizabeth Estiel June 12, 1848. She was born January 28, 1820. They had four children, Martha E., Robert H., William Mack and Charles H. June 22, 1856, while working at a saw mill his team became frightened at the blowing of the whistle, ran away dragging a sawlog over him, which caused his death.

T. E. Cantrall, only son of Young M. Cantrall, son of Thomas, son of Levi, was born near Fancy Prairie, Illinois, March 12, 1862. His father was born April 30, 1836. February 14, 1861, he married Mary E. Graham, of Athens, Ill. They lived on a farm until 1862. He enlisted in Company C, 114th Illinois Infantry, and died at Vicksburg, July 1, 1863. Thomas E. Cantrall married Grace May Whitney May 8, 1883. Their children are: Estella May, Young Albert, Clie Joseph, Allen Whitney and Paul Graham. Mr. Cantrall has taught school for a number of years. His mother lives at Athens, Ill.

Charles S. Cantrall.   Harriet A. Cantrall.

Charles S. Cantrall, son of Levi, was born January 6, 1826, near Cantrall, Ill. He grew to manhood on his father's farm. When he was five years old he fell from a rail fence and hurt his left leg which caused a white swelling. After years of suffering, his leg was amputated. Mr. Cantrall was married three times. First to Emily M. Vandergrift. Two children were born to them, and she died, and he married Lucy A. Swearengen. One child was born, and she died. April 26, 1855, Mr. Cantrall married Harriet A. Graham. She was born February 17, 1826, in Athens, Illinois. Her father, Peter Graham, came to Illinois, in 1829. He was born in New York City. When 23 years old went to North Carolina, then to New Orleans, where he lived three years. Lived in Athens, Ill., 62 years, dying in his 91st year. To them were born ten children. The father died December 18, 1885. Charles Cantrall was radical on the temperance question. He was a member of the Christian Church more than 40 years. He was a Mason, being a member of the Masonic Order for more than 30 years before his death.

Stephen Oscar Price.

Mary Ellen Price.

Mary E. Cantrall, daughter of Charles S., son of Levi, was born January 13, 1848, in Sangamon county, Illinois. January 25, 1866, she was married to Stephen O. Price. He was born January 24, 1847, in Athens. His parents came from Baltimore, Maryland, in 1838. When he was about 10 years of age his parents moved to a farm one and one-half miles northeast of Athens, Ill., where he grew to manhood. After he was married he moved to a farm east of Athens, and from there to a farm he owns four miles east of Lincoln, Ill., in 1867, where they now live. Their children are: Emily Ellen and William Oscar. W. O. Price was born May 29, 1870. Emily E. married A. F. Reed March 14, 1889, and lives at Bement, Ill. William O. Price married Lyda Section November 24, 1892.

McDonald Cantrall.   Henry Augustus Cantrall

McDonald Cantrall, son of Charles S., son of Levi, was born August 20, 1851, near Cantrall, Ill. His mother died when he was three months old. His father moved to a farm near Illiopolis, Ill., in 1866. August 4, 1870, he married Margaret M. Peden, of Illiopolis. She was born January 14, 1851. They lived on a farm near there until May, 1897, when they moved to Illiopolis. Mr. Cantrall still manages the farm and also is postmaster at Illiopolis. Their children are: Maud A., Henry A., Bruce T., Josiah P., Beatrix M., Tracey E. Maud married G. M. Mathews January 21, 1894. They live in Illiopolis. Tracey was killed September 7, 1895, by a wagon running over her.

H. A. Cantrall, son of McDonald, was born February 9, 1874. Mr. Cantrall was born and raised on a farm. In the spring of 1898 he and a friend started west, got as far as Fort Crook, Neb., where troops were being enlisted for the Spanish war. They both enlisted in Company A, 22d Nebraska Infantry. They went to Cuba, and he was in the thickest of the battle at Santiago, returning home September 1, 1898. He says that although the shot was as thick as hail about him for hours, he came out without a scratch.

Charles Henry Cantrall.   Viola Cantrall.

Charles H. Cantrall, son of Charles, son of Levi, was born
March 12, 1856. He was raised on a farm two miles south
of Cantrall, Ill. When he was 12 years old his father moved
to a farm two miles west of Illiopolis, Ill., where he grew to
manhood. In 1884 he went to Kansas, where he engaged in
business. In 1894 he returned to St. Louis, Mo., where he
lived one year, then moved to Athens, Ill. April 28, 1898, he
was married to Viola Batterton, of Athens, Ill. Her father,
Elijah Batterton, is an old settler, living near Salisbury, Ill.
Mr. Cantrall, with his brother, Thomas D., is engaged in the
grocery business in Athens, Ill. He is a member of the In-
dependent Order of Odd Fellows.

John W. Cantrall, M. D.

Allie Cantrall.

Dr. J. W. Cantrall, son of Charles S., son of Levi, was born April 8, 1863, near Cantrall, Ill. He grew to manhood on his father's farm. When a boy he attended District School and in 1891 he entered the College of Physicians and Surgeons in St. Louis, Mo. He commenced the practice of medicine in Mt. Auburn, Ill., and in 1896 he moved to Buffalo, Ill. There he married Alura V. Prephater April 29, 1896. In the spring of 1898 he moved to Rochester, Ill.

Allie Cantrall, daughter of Charles S. Cantrall, son of Levi, was born January 14, 1861, near Cantrall, Ill. When she was eight years old her parents moved to a farm two miles north of Illiopolis, Ill. Since her father's death she and her brother, Ira, has lived with their mother on the old home place. She is a member of the Christian Church at Illiopolis, Ill.

Joshua L. Cantrall.   Rebecca Cantrall.

J. L. Cantrall, son of Levi, was born July 28, 1828, in
Sangamon county, Illinois. He grew to manhood on a farm.
October 16, 1847, was married to Rebecca Hedrick. She was
born October 8, 1828, in Kentucky. Her parents were among
the early settlers in Sangamon county. Joshua moved to
Sigourney, Iowa, in 1864, but returned to Illinois in 1866, and
bought a farm one and one-half miles west of Illiopolis, where
he died March 17, 1882. He was a charter member of Illio
polis Lodge, A. F. & A. M., No. 521. He was an elder in the
Christian Church for fifteen years. Was a member more than
30 years. He and his wife were great workers in the church.
He was a radical temperance worker. There were thirteen
children. His widow has lived in Illiopolis for the past five
years.

LaFayette Cantrall.   Gussie Cantrall.

LaFayette Cantrall, son of Joshua L., son of Levi, was born January 16, 1849, in Sangamon county. When 15 years old his parents moved to Iowa, but returned in 1866. July 23, 1874, was married to Gussie Chambers. She was born April 11, 1856, near Augusta, Ala. Her father, Thomas Chambers, was a noted physician; he also was Captain in the Southern army. Her mother's maiden name was Charlotte Norman of a noted family in the south. In 1878 LaFayette went to Kansas and stayed one year, returned to farm three and one-half miles west of Illiopolis, where he has a comfortable home.

Barton R. Cantrall.   William H. Cantrall.

B. R. Cantrall, son of Joshua L., son of Levi, was born April 26, 1856, in Sangamon county, Illinois, on a farm. In 1878 he went to Kansas, staying about one year. Came back to Illinois, and in 1884 went to Colorado. From there to Old Mexico, then to St. Louis, where he lived six years. Held a responsible position in the penitentiary at Joliet in 1881; was there when Garfield died. Attended school at Valparaiso, Ind., in 1882. Since then has lived Illiopolis, Ill., and engaged in farming. Mr. Cantrall is a member of the Masonic Order. Is single and makes his home with his mother.

W. H. Cantrall, son of Charles, son of Levi, was born November 28, 1867, near Illiopolis on a farm, where he grew to manhood. March 1, 1895, married Nannie Muir, at Illiopolis. Ill. They moved to Brunswick, Mo., where they lived on a farm. At this writing he is preparing to move in December, 1898, to his brother Thomas' farm, just north of Illiopolis, his brother moving to Athens and engaging in the grocery business there with his brother, Charles H. Mr. Cantrall is a member of the Knights of Pythias Lodge.

James Hardy Council.   Julia Ann Council.

Julia Ann Cantrall, daughter of Joshua L., son of Levi, was born April 11, 1860, near Cantrall, Ill. Her parents moved to a farm near Illiopolis, Ill. There she was married to James H. Council December 5, 1883. He was born January 4, 1859, on the farm, where his father, John Council, still lives and has lived since 1851, three miles northwest of Sherman, Ill. His father is now 76 years old and lives within one-half mile of where he was born. In the spring of 1882 J. H. Council moved to the farm his father gave him, one mile west of Elkhart, Ill., where he has since lived. They have four children: John Russell, born April 2, 1885; Hardy Edna, born May 1, 1890; LaFayette McDonald, born July 27, 1892; Clara Florence, born December 15, 1893. Mr. Council and wife are among the earnest workers of the Christian Church at Elkhart.

McDonald Cantrall.   Clara P. Campbell.

McDonald Cantrall, son of Joshua L., son of Levi, was born January 1, 1862. He lived with his mother in Illiopolis, Ill., and was a farmer. April 26, 1898, he enlisted in the 5th Ill. Cavalry, Troop D, and went with the company to Chickamauga, but they were never permitted to go to the field of battle and since the close of the war have been mustered out and sent home. Thus, at least two of the name Cantrall, McDonald and his cousin, Henry Augustus, enlisted in the late war. Others who are connected with the family, as you will see, went also. The picture above was taken at Chickamauga. His company was brought to Fort Sheridan about August 20, and he arrived at Springfield September 6.

Clara P. Cantrall, daughter of Joshua, son of Levi, was born September 8, 1866. Married Charles J. Campbell, December 5, 1888. He was born March 29, 1859. Their children: Owen Henry, born September 12, 1889; Helen, born September 16, 1895. They live on a farm near Illiopolis, Ill.

Jesse Cantrall.

Jesse Cantrall, son of Levi, was born April 7, 1830. Married Eliza J. Humes. Enlisted August, 1862, for three years in Company C, 114th Illinois Infantry. He was commissioned Second Lieutenant at the organization, was promoted to Captain and served as such until the end of the Rebellion, and was honorably discharged. He was slightly wounded during the war and has been a cripple for many years from the effect of a gun wound in one arm, since the war. He moved to Kansas in 1868, camped where the Stock Yards now are in Kansas City, and was offered 160 acres of land there for $6 per acre. He lives now 25 miles southwest from Kansas City, Mo., at Olathe, Kan. Their children are: Martha Rachel, Jefferson, Ann, Fannie E., Mary Jane, Johnnie, Ella, Jesse, Cora, Ida, Joshua.

McDonald Cantrall.   Narcissus Cantrall.

McDonald Cantrall, son of Levi Cantrall, was born
April 5, 1833, in Sangamon county, Illinois. He married Narcissus Hedrick, March 29, 1854. She was born
May 15, 1864, near Buffalo Hart, Ill. Her parents were Jon-
athan and Julia Hedrick, who moved to Buffalo Hart Grove,
Ill., in the fall of 1830. McDonald Cantrall moved on a farm
one mile south of Cantrall, Ill. From there he moved to a
farm four and one-half miles northeast of Cantrall, Ill., where
he died September 16, 1872. Their only child, Charles, was
born February 14, 1855. Mr. Cantrall was an enthusiastic
farmer and lived on one of the best farms in the county. His
widow and son have lived there since his death.

Charles Cantrall.   Florence Cantrall.

Charles Cantrall, son of McDonald, son of Levi, was born February 11, 1855, on the farm one mile south of Cantrall, Ill. Soon after his birth his parents moved to a farm four and one-half miles northeast of Cantrall. His father died when he was 17 years old. He was the only child and with his mother managed the farm which his father left them. May 16, 1888, he married Florence Council. She was born June 4, 1867. She was the daughter of John H. and Edna Council. They have two children, John Harvey, born May 4, 1889, and McDonald, born February 2, 1897. Mr. Cantrall is a member of Van Meter Lodge 762, A. F. and A. M., and of Floral Lodge No. 647, I. O. O. F., at Athens, Ill.

Henry C. Graham.   Fannie L. Graham.

Fannie L. Cantrall, daughter of Levi, was born October 9, 1838, near Cantrall, Ill. Married Henry C. Graham, January 6, 1857. He was born May 8, 1833, at Athens, Ill. His father, Peter Graham, came from New York City to Illinois in 1829. He lived in Athens, Ill., 62 years, dying in his 91st year. The year Mr. Graham was married they moved to a farm five miles east of Athens, Ill., where they still live. Their children are: Mary A., William H., Arminta, Joseph S. and Carrie. Their children are all married and live near them. Mr. Cantrall and his wife are members of the M. E. Church at Athens, Ill. Mr. Graham is a carpenter by trade, but has turned his attention to farming for many years.

Joseph S. Cantrall.

Joseph S. Cantrall, son of Levi, was born October 16, 1841. Married Margaret A. Canterbury, daughter of J. T. Canterbury, January 14, 1869. He became a cattle merchant when 19 years old. Was successful until the war times when he and a partner bought 1,000 head of cattle, which they shipped at a heavy loss, caused by closing of the civil war. He was in New York City in February, 1865, and saw cattle sell for 28 cents per pound net. The highest price at which cattle were ever sold. He remained in the cattle business until 1872. In 1871 he built a grain elevator at Cantrall, which he operated for 16 years. He was nominated in 1886 by the Republican party of Sangamon county for office of Sheriff. He ran 1,000 votes ahead of his ticket, but it is believed that the returns were changed, counting him out by only 60 votes. He was renominated for the same office in 1890. Ran 1,350 votes ahead of the ticket, the county going Democratic by 1,700 votes. The next year he went to Nebraska as agent for a grain firm. Returned to Springfield in 1894. He is now General Special Agent for the Northwestern Mutual Life Insurance Company, and doing a growing business.

Wyatt Cantrall.   William M. Cantrall.

Wyatt Cantrall, son of Joshua Cantrall, was born December 20, 1790, in Kentucky. There he was married to Sally England, and moved to Clark county, Ohio. In company with Mrs. Cantrall's father, Stephen England, they moved to St. Clair county, Ill., in the fall of 1818. In the spring of 1819 they moved to Sangamon county. His wife was born December 20, 1794. Wyatt and Levi married sisters. His brother, Levi, came in the fall of 1819. These brothers lived on adjoining farms just north of where the town of Cantrall is, for 20 years. Then Wyatt moved to Sterling, Ill., where his wife died August 4, 1840. He married Mrs. Polly Kingsbury, whose maiden name was Foster. They had one son, Joshua P. Mrs. Cantrall died about 1859, and Wyatt moved to Kansas, and died October 25, 1877.

W. M. Cantrall, son of William G., was born December 28, 1822, in Ohio. Came to Illinois with his parents in 1824. They lived on a farm two miles south of Cantrall, Ill., April 3, 1845. He married Adaline Claywell. He enlisted August 12, 1862, for three years in Co. C, 114th Ill. Inf. Disease was brought on by over-exertion at the Battle of Guntown, Mississippi, June 10, 1864. He died in the hospital at Memphis, Tenn., July 9, 1864. He was a member of the Christian Church. His widow lives near Lyons, Rice county, Kansas.

Samuel Denny Cantrall.   Sarah S. Cantrall.

S. D. Cantrall, oldest son of Wyatt, was born born February 9, 1816, in Ohio. Came to Illinois with his parents, and March 6, 1837, married Sarah S. Alexander. She was born November 7, 1820, in Kentucky. John Alexander, her father, came from Kentucky to Illinois, in 1826. Samuel D. moved to Rock River and lived eight years; then to a farm two miles east of Athens, Ill., where he died May 1, 1884. Since which time his widow has made her home with her son, Henry. They were members of the Christian Church. Their children are: Albert A., Wyatt E., Mary H., John S., Lucinda S., Henry, Eliza, Margaret A.

Albert A. Cantrall.   Wiott E. Cantrall.

Albert A. Cantrall, son of Samuel D., son of Wiott, was born November 15, 1839. Married Martha Hurt March 6, 1862. There were no children, and his widow lives in Athens, Ill. He enlisted August 12, 1862, in Company C, 114th Illinois Infantry for three years, and was appointed Sergeant. He was captured at the battle of Guntown, Miss., in June, 1864, and was placed in Andersonville prison, where he remained about five months, and after that was taken from one prison to another to prevent being released by the Union force. Was paroled March 1, 1865, and died of starvation and exposure March 2, 1865, at Wilmington, N. C.

Wiott E. Cantrall, son of Samuel D., son of Wyatt, was born November 5, 1841, in Whiteside county, Ill. Moved to Menard county when quite young. Grew to manhood on a farm. November 17, 1869, married Grizilla Holland. She was born in Kentucky, April 9, 1848. They lived on a farm near Athens, Ill., for 20 years, during which time three children were born to them. Annie Bell, Ina May, Hattie Slone. In 1889 they moved to Cantrall, living there one year. Then moved to Springfield, Ill., where Mr. Cantrall died March 31, 1898. His widow lives in Springfield, Ill.

David P. Cantrall.   Henry Cantrall.

D. P. Cantrall, son of Wyatt, was born May 7, 1818, in
Ohio. That year his parents moved to Sangamon county,
Illinois. March 13, 1841, he married Eleanor McLemore. She
was born March 20, 1820. Their children are: Young M.,
Sarah E., Erastus D., Catherine E. Y. M. Cantrall lives at
Milledgeville, Ill. Mrs. Catherine Riddle lives near Rushville,
Neb. The other two died young. Mrs. Cantrall died Janu-
ary 15, 1864, and David P. married for his second wife Ursula
Bull January 15, 1861. Their children are: Eddie C., Wyatt
B. and Nettie C. Mrs. Eddie C. Kirkpatrick lives near Lis-
bon, Iowa. Wyatt B. lives near Stanborn, Iowa. Mrs. Net-
tie C. Whiteman near Lisbon, Iowa. David P. Cantrall died
January 21, 1892, and his widow died August 25, 1894.

Henry Cantrall, son of Samuel D., son of Wyatt, was
born February 28, 1849, on the farm where he now lives, two
miles east of Athens, Ill. January 1, 1873, he married Emma
E. Graham. She was born September 6, 1853, in Athens, Ill.
Their children are: Alvin W., Arthur W., Verna E., Samuel
D. Alvin married Allie Langford and lives in Springfield,
Ill. Henry Cantrall and his wife are members of the Chris-
tian Church at Athens, Ill. He is a member of Floral Lodge
647, I. O. O. F., at Athens, Ill. Also a member of the Home
Forum and Court of Honor Life Insurance Orders.

William Cantrill.

W. Cantrill, son of Thomas Cantrill, was born in Green county, Kentucky, January 17, 1800. Moved to Springfield, Ill., March, 1825. February 14, 1828, he married Elizabeth Hall. She was born in Kentucky December 18, 1809. They moved to Decatur, Ill., in 1833. He brought the first stock of merchandise to Decatur and opened the first store in that place. Ex-Governor Richard J. Oglesby was his first clerk. He was the first postmaster in Decatur; was a member of the Legislature 1854-55, and served three terms as County Treasurer; was always a staunch Democrat and for many years was a leader of the party in that section. He died November 26, 1881, in Decatur. His children are: Thomas Hall, Jane Ellen, Mary Elizabeth, Susan Lavinia. Thomas H. married and went west and was accidentally drowned. Jane E. married Dr. A. L. Keller. She died in October, 1892. Mary E. married William Dillon. She died October 26, 1883. Susan L. married Harland P. Christie. She is the only child living and her home is 231 Madison street, Brooklyn Borough, New York City.

Joel Cantrill.   Zerilda Cantrill.

Joel Cantrill, son of Thomas, was born January 8, 1811, in Kentucky. Came to Illinois with his parents in 1828. They settled four and one-half miles east of where Springfield now is. May 16, 1839, married Zerilda E. Branch. She was born November 19, 1831. Her parents came to Illinois from Kentucky in 1830, and settled seven miles east of Springfield, where they lived and died. Their children are: Louis M., Edward T., William D., James N., Laura Jane, Henrietta, Henry A. (twins), Emily B., Charles, Benjamin H. Joel Cantrill enlisted in the Mexican war, but was never called into service. He died September 4, 1866. His widow lives with her children.

ABRAHAM LINCOLN

As he appeared 1860. Said to be the most correct likeness
of the martyred president.

THE LINCOLN HOME AT SPRINGFIELD
Corner Eighth and Jackson Streets.

NATIONAL LINCOLN MONUMENT AT SPRINGFIELD

BIRDSEYE VIEW ILLINOIS STATE FAIR GROUNDS AT SPRINGFIELD

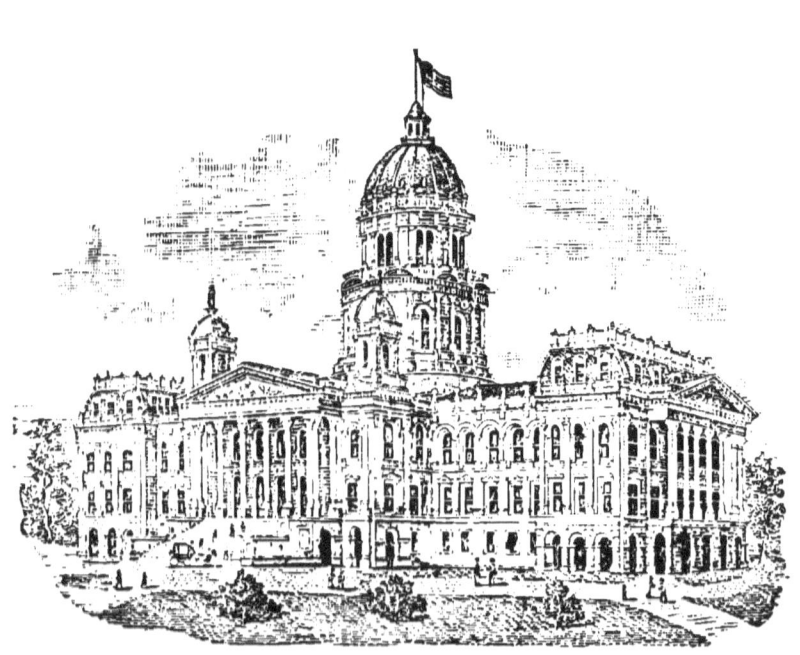

THE ILLINOIS CAPITOL AT SPRINGFIELD

FAMILY RECORD.

The Cantrell family is of Welch, Scotch, and Irish descent. Zebulon Cantrell came from Wales to America about the year 1700. Some say that two brothers came with him, but of this I find no record. You will find several families at the close of this record, whose ancestors I cannot trace. It is claimed that Zebulon Cantrell built the first brick house in Philadelphia, Pennsylvania.

He had a son Joseph, and Joseph had a son Joshua. Joshua's grandson, John S., of Derby, Kansas, has the original evidence that he took out naturalization papers.

> Pittsylvania County. I do hereby certify that Joshua Cantril, oath taken and subscribed the oath or affirmation of allegiance and fidelity, as directed by an act of General Assembly, entitled, An act to oblige the free male inhabitants of this state above a certain age to give assurance of allegiance [SEAL.] to the same, and for other purposes. Witness my hand and seal this 6th day of September, 1777.
>
> J. L. MORTON.

JOSHUA CANTRELL was a soldier in the war for American Independence. He was born in Pennsylvania, but moved to Virginia, then to Kentucky in 1789. He was the father of nine sons, but no daughter. Four of his sons died without families, the other five married in Kentucky and moved to Ohio, then to Illinois. There were born to them 64 children, 33 sons and 31 daughters.

The copy of the record given below is not complete, but is just as my great grandfather made it.

FAMILY RECORD.
OF BIRTHS AND DEATHS IN THE FAMILY OF JOSHUA CANTRELL,

To the present time, 1829, including a period of eighty-one years.

Joshua Cantrell, born August 8, 1748—Died September 9, 1800.

Ann Graham, alias Cantrell, his wife, born May 3, 1751—Died February 19, 1819.

From whom descended:

1st. Zebulon G. Cantrell, born June 29, 1773—Died. Whose wife was Sarah McCollam, born February 8, 1779.

From whom descended:

Ann Cantrell, born August 31, 1798—Died May 16, 1822.

Polly Cantrell, born July 29, 1800.

Joshua Cantrell, born April 3, 1802.

Chrispan Cantrell, born February 29, 1804.

Agnes Minerva Cantrell, born September 12, 1806.

John McCollam Cantrell, born February 22, 1808.

James Madison Cantrell, born April 10, 1810.

Sarah Cantrell, born March 14, 1812.

Zebulon Pike Cantrell, born January 17, 1814.

Eliza Cantrell, born July 4, 1816.

Rebecca and Rachel Cantrell, born July 25, 1818.

Wyatt Cantrell, born May 11, 1821.

William Levi Cantrell, born May 15, 1823.

2d. James Cantrell, born August 24, 1775—Died August 24, 1778.

3d. Christopher Cantrell, born May 16, 1778.

4th. Joshua Cantrell, born April 3, 1779. Whose wife was Rachel McCollam, born April 2, 1781.

From whom descended:

Elizabeth Cantrell, born February 27, 1800.

Jane Cantrell, born August 4, 1801.

Thirza Cantrell, born Dec. 25, 1802.

Zebulon Cantrell, born August 24, 1805.

Mahala Cantrell, born July 1, 1807.

Polly Cantrell, born February 8, 1810.

William Cantrell, born April 1, 1812.

Levi Cantrell, born May 6, 1814.

Nancy Cantrell, born June 13, 1816.

Joshua Christopher Cantrell, born September 20, 1818.

Seth Cantrell, born August 25, 1821.

Eli Cantrell, born February 6, 1824.

Rachel Cantrell, born April 23, 1826.

5th.   Thomas Carsey Cantrell, born October 11, 1782.—
Died September 30, 1797.

6th.   William G. Cantrell, born September 6, 1784.

Whose wife was Deborah Metz, born November 16, 1785.
   From whom descended:

Dorothy Cantrell, born March 15, 1805.

Ann Cantrell, born August 1, 1806.

Elizabeth Cantrell, born August 29, 1808.

Joshua M. Cantrell, born December 17, 1810.

Thirza Cantrell, born November 8, 1812.

Adam M. Cantrell, born February 27, 1815.

Deborah Cantrell, born February 16, 1817.

Mahala Cantrell, born December 4, 1818.

Susannah Cantrell, born November 23, 1820.

William M. Cantrell, born December 28, 1822.

Maranda Cantrell, born May 12, 1826.

Andrew Jackson Cantrell, born January 4, 1829.

7th.   Levi Cantrell, born October 1, 1787.

Whose wife was Fanny England, born October 2, 1792.
   From whom descended:

Thomas Cantrell, born October 11, 1810.

Ann Cantrell, born July 17, 1812.

Nancy Cantrell, born November 13, 1813.

Stephen L. Cantrell, born April 4, 1815.

Celindra Cantrell, born November 14, 1816.

Eleanor Cantrell, born October 17, 1818.

Elizabeth E. Cantrell, born May 26, 1820.

Levi L. Cantrell, born March 17, 1822.

Rachel Cantrell, born February 8, 1824.

Charles S. Cantrell, born January 6, 1826.

Joshua L. Cantrell, born July 28, 1828.

8th. Wyatt Cantrell, born December 20, 1790.
Whose wife was Sally England, born November 2, 1794.
   From whom descended:
Eliza Cantrell, born September 8, 1813.
Samuel Denny Cantrell, born February 9, 1816.
David P. Cantrell, born May 7, 1818.
Zebulon E. Cantrell, born August 11, 1823.
Wyatt E. Cantrell, born March 22, 1835.
Stephen England Cantrell, born April 20, 1827.
   9th.   Samuel Cantrell, born February 3, 1793.—Died July 24, 1795.

When this you see remember me.—ZEBULON G. CANTRELL.

DeWitt County, Ill., May 14, 1841.

My Dear Children:

Before you see this I shall have gone the way of all the living to that world from whose bourne no traveler returns. This therefore as my last legasee, though not least, I have thought proper to leave to you all in common and it is my last and solemn request that you may bear it in mind and act accordingly.

In the first place I will say, remember your Creator in the days of your youth, the evil days come not when you shall or may say I have no pleasure in them, by so doing you will be enabled in the next place, to live honestly, righteously and soberly in this present world and sure of a blessed reward in that which is to come.

It is my hope and request that you lead honest and peaceable lives, avoiding as much as possible all broils of every sort, but on the other hand cultivate honorable friendship, don't let little things interrupt your good feeling toward your neighbors, but more especially amongst yourselves.

I have seen broils among brothers and sisters and oh! how hateful.   I do sincerely hope this may not be the case with you.   We are all fallible and are liable to do wrong, though as we need forgiveness, it is our duty to forgive.

I want you as a band of brothers to be friendly and work to each others hand and if one should be more prosperous than another do not envy him, nor let him that is prosperous look down on his poor brother.   Let not, as is sometimes the

case, any little frivolous difference about the little property
I may leave mar your good feeling toward each other.

I have done as near equally by you all as I could. If I
have failed in judgment, it has not been because I preferred
one before another of you.

The foregoing I wrote in much pain as you will see and
remember by the date, and although it is very short I could
not have given utterance to this much had you have been all
present. My feelings in such a case would have failed me.
Therefore I have left this little thing as a memorial of my
tender regard and parental feelings for those I have been the
means of bringing into the world, and for whom I now pray
may be preserved and inclined and enabled to fulfill this,
my requirements, with every other duty that may be incum-
bent upon them.

And now, my children, I bid you farewell and may the
God of peace have you in his holy keeping and may you set
the determination to say and do as Joshua of old—let others
do as they please; as for me and my house we will serve the
Lord.   ZEBULON G. CANTRELL.

Alike to all my children, both natural and adopted.

June 25, 1843, DeWitt County, Illinois.
When I am pained and sore distressed,
And I call to mind I once was blessed,
With one soft hand to hold my head,
But now that hand lies cold and dead.
Within that lonely sacred spot,
By all but me perhaps forgot.
Entombed here lies beneath this willow,
The hand that often smoothed my pillow
When racked with pain and sore distressed,
Of earthly friends she was the best.
                                    ZEBULON G. CANTRELL.

Toast for July 4th, 1845:
In friendship we're met, in friendship let's part,
Let nothing but friendship have place in our heart;
And in duty and friendship let each of us vie
Till we meet here again on the Fourth of July.
                                    ZEBULON G. CANTRELL.

ZEBULON G. CANTRELL.

The oldest son of Joshua, was born June 29, 1773. Married Sarah McCollam August 31, 1797. She was born February 8, 1779. They moved to Ohio in 1811, and in 1833 moved to Sangamon county, Ill. In 1834 moved to DeWitt county, Illinois. They had 14 children: Ann, Polly, Joshua, Chrispan, Agnes Minerva, John McCollam, James Madison, Sarah, Zebulon Pike, Eliza, Rebecca and Rachel; twins, Wyatt, William Levi.

Their mother died May 26, 1843, and their father September 11, 1845, both near Waynesville, Ill.

ANN CANTRELL

Was born August 31, 1798; died May 16, 1822. Married John Branson September 12, 1817. Mr. Branson was a teamster during the war of 1812, and had his hand crippled while on duty. They had one child, ZEBULON, who was born June 20, 1818. Married Rachel Brancher August 6, 1840. She was born March 10, 1821. They had 11 children, 6 of whom died when young; the other 5 are: Emily, Caroline, Isaac R., Charles Marion, Zebulon Seigle.

EMILY BRANSON was born October 29, 1843. Married Dilworth B. Carter October 29, 1861. They had 5 children: Harry Dilworth, Stella E., Irving Robbins, and two died young. Mr. Carter lives at Omaha, Neb.

CAROLINE BRANSON was born May 26, 1848. Married James C. Brown. They have one child, Blanche Iola, and live at Atlantic, Iowa.

ISAAC R. BRANSON was born January 28, 1851. Married Mida A. Bishop. They have no children, and live at Aurora, Neb.

CHARLES M. BRANSON was born July 19, 1853. Married Ida D. Currier August 22, 1877. They have 4 children: Lois,

Stewart, born May 23, 1878; Bernice Marie, born December 31, 1882; Charles Blaine, born January 28, 1884; Joe Brancher, born June 1, 1886. Mr. Branson is a farmer and stock raiser at Lincoln, Neb.

ZEBULON S. BRANSON, born March 25, 1862. Married Anna B. Vaughn in 1885. They have 4 children: Charles, Milton, Leo Burnell, Zebulon Dorr, John McKinley. Mr. Branson is a farmer and stock raiser and live stock auctioneer at Waverly, Neb.

Zebulon Branson enlisted in 1862, in the 103d Illinois Infantry for three years. He was First Lieutenant, and was killed June 27, 1864, while leading his company in a charge on the rebel fortifications at Kenesaw Mountain.

POLLY CANTRELL

Was born July 29, 1800, and died while young.

JOSHUA E. CANTRELL

Was born April 3, 1802. Died October 27, 1860. Married Eliza Scott July 31, 1828. She was born October 18, 1801. They had two children: Sarah and John S.

SARAH CANTRELL was born May 31, 1829. Marreid Irvin Danels February 17, 1848. He was born August 11, 1825. Died May 19, 1898. They had 9 children: William, John, Edward, Hannah, Jeremiah Perry, Eliza, Ida, Lydia, Mary A., Cara.

William Danels was born May 15, 1849. Married Mary Eliza Mills August 19, 1869. She was born November 22, 1850. Their children are: Omer, born September 25, 1871; Charles W. was born December 6, 1872. Married Lulu McKinney June 20, 1897. They live at Delta, Iowa. Frank born September 30, 1874; Irvin, Jr., born December 28, 1885; Juanita was born August 31, 1887. Artemas S. was born November 11, 1892. Died December 8, 1892.

Mr. Danels is a farmer and lives at Batavia, Iowa.

John Danels, born June 24, 1851. Died September 17, 1851.

Edward Danels was born July 8, 1853. Married Sophronia E. Jenkins March 28, 1878. She was born August 2, 1858. Their children are: Claude H., born January 20, 1879; Jesse L., born March 28, 1882. Married Nason Kellogg March 28, 1898. Mr. Danels is a farmer and lives near Clinton, Illinois.

Hannah Danels was born April 7, 1856. Married S. M. Swartz July 22, 1885. He was born April 27, 1859. Their children are: Fanny Fay, born May 9, 1886; Mamie J., born September 7, 1887; Ben Harrison, born November 19, 1888; Reuben DeWitt, born December 20, 1890. They live at Parnell, Illinois.

J. P. Danels was born August 8, 1858. Married Addie M. Robertson March 15, 1885. She was born March 9, 1868. Died July 4, 1886. October 20, 1892. Mr. Danels married Fanny C. Lewis. She was born August 29, 1857. Mr. Danels runs a dray line in Clinton, Illinois.

Eliza A. Danels was born December 8, 1861. Died March 15, 1862.

Ida Danels was born September 9, 1863, and lives with her mother on the home place, 6 miles southeast of Waynesville, Illinois.

Lyda Ann was born January 31, 1867. Died March 3, 1867.

M. Cara Danels was born December 8, 1868. Married William McCrary February 26, 1890. He was born November 28, 1860. Their children are: D. Russel, born July 5, 1891; infant daughter born November 18, 1894; Nilla B., born August 22, 1896. Mr. McCrary is a carpenter and lives at Waynesville, Ill.

John S. Cantrell was born November 10, 1832. Married Lucy S. Martin May 3, 1859. She was born October 6, 1840. Their children are: Anna E., born October 3, 1860. Married F. L. Moon October 16, 1878. They have three children: Charlie Claude, born December 8, 1879; Lillian Lucretia, born June 16, 1881; Love N. Tangle, born September 26, 1883; died June 14, 1885. Mr. Moon died and his widow married G. E.

Atchison July 2, 1890. They have one child, Pauline Ester, born July 20, 1894. They live in Wichita, Kan.

Joshua Boyd was born June 24, 1865. Married Ella G. Reeder September 27, 1887. Their children are: Victor L., Paul K., Ernest G. Mr. Cantrell is a farmer and lives at Current View, Mo. Mary B., born February 8, 1867. Died November 25, 1869. Samuel H., born March 26, 1871. Died March 16, 1874.

Florence H., born April 10, 1877. Died March 1, 1879. John S. Cantrell was a soldier in the late war, as shown by the following certificate of gallant and meritorious conduct:

This is to certify that John S. Cantril has served in Company F, 38th Regiment Illinois Infantry Volunteers, exchanging the comforts and endearments of home for the hardships and perils of a soldier's life. He was mustered in the service of the United States to serve in the war against the great Rebellion, on the 15th day of August, 1861, and by his soldierly bearing and gallant conduct has won the respect of his officers and is entitled to the gratitude of his country.

LEMUEL K. WESTCOTT,
1st Lieut. and Adjt. 38th Reg. Ill. Infantry Volunteers, Bridgeport, Alabama, Jan. 22, 1864.

Discharged September 15, 1864, at Chattanooga, Tenn., by expiration of term of service.

Mr. Cantrell now lives on a farm near Derby, Kansas, and is a carpenter by trade.

CHRISPAN CANTRELL

Was born February 29, 1804, and died while young.

AGNES MINERVA CANTRELL

Was born September 12, 1806. Married John McIntyre. I have been unable to get the history of this family. I am told that all the children died before their mother, and that there are some grandchildren living near Fort Dodge, Kansas. Mrs. McIntyre died at her brother William's home in Kenney, Illinois.

JOHN McCOLLAM CANTRELL.

Was born February 22, 1808. Died January 27, 1862. Married Joanna M. Jones November 18, 1830. She was born September 11, 1812. Died September 28, 1870. They moved from Ohio to Sangamon county, Illinois, in 1831, and in 1834 to Waynesville, DeWitt county, Illinois. They had 12 children: William J., Zebulon D., Elizabeth, Ira J., Mary, Miles Trotter, Alma, Alma J., John E., Albert, Evaline, Marcus.

WILLIAM J. CANTRALL was born September 24, 1831. Died April 17, 1896. Married Lora Amelia Hickox February 14, 1856. She was born May 24, 1837. Died February 14, 1871. They had three children: Frederick Augustus, Nellie Viola, Francis Amelia.

Frederick A. Cantrall was born February 9, 1857. Married Mary E. Teeter January 19, 1878. She was born March 21, 1858. Their children are: Lora E., born May 20, 1879; David Teeter, born January 10, 1881, died September 10, 1881; Eva Vista, born October 7, 1882; Frederick Ormsby, born July 7, 1887. Mr. Cantral is a printer and lives in Denver, Col.

Nellie V. Cantrall was born in 1865, and died in infancy.

Frances A. Cantrall was born May 26, 1861, in Waynesville, Illinois. She received her earlier education chiefly in the public schools of Emporia, Kansas, and Lincoln, Illinois. She went to Chicago in 1885 and took the course in the Illinois Training School for Nurses. Graduated from that institution in 1887. In 1889 she entered the Northwestern University, Woman's Medical School, and took her degree of Doctor of Medicine in 1893. At the close of that same year she located at Evansville, Indiana, where she has since engaged in the practice of medicine.

William J. Cantrall married for his second wife Miss Mary E. Gilbert, March 20, 1884, at Lincoln, Illinois. They moved to Dakota, where she died April 12, 1885. He married for his third wife the widowed sister of his second wife, Mrs. Emma Clark, April 15, 1886, in Chicago, Illinois. His widow lives in Detroit, Minnesota.

ZEBULON DANIEL CANTRELL was born August 28, 1833. Died May 16, 1897. Married Susan Foreman December 13, 1855. They had five children: Carmi G., Joanna J., Elmer E., Thomas D., and Martha A. Mrs. Cantrall was born March 21, 1835, and lives in Clinton, Illinois.

C. G. Cantrell was born April 19, 1857. Married Mary O. Bell January 1, 1879. She was born June 4, 1860. They had five children: Dora Imo, born December 19, 1880; Anna May, born September 27, 1882; Guy Leslie, born October 18, 1885; Ada Luella, born November 16, 1891, died May 28, 1893; Carmi Miles, born November 1, 1894. Mr. Cantrell is a minister in the Christian church and lives at Irvington, Indiana.

Joanna J. Cantrell was born June 13, 1859. Died February 27, 1882. Married D. W. Lanterman June 12, 1878. They had one child, Nina Wenona, born March 31, 1880. She was raised by her mother's parents and still lives with her Grandmother Cantrell. Mr. Lanterman married Cora Wallace and lives at Broken Bow, Neb.

E. E. Cantrell was born August 21, 1861. Married Jennie E. Britten December 24, 1884. She was born April 27, 1861. They have five children: Raper Z., born November 14, 1885; Floyd S., born November 26, 1887; Alma F., born June 23, 1890; Mary Abbie, born February 24, 1892; Jennie Lelah, born April 12, 1896. Mr. Cantrell is a farmer and lives on the old home place, four and one-half miles southeast of Waynesville, Illinois.

T. D. Cantrell was born February 3, 1864. Married Marietta Arnett August 31, 1887. She was born March 26, 1866. Their children are: Leta Fern, born February 21, 1889; Leona Fay, born November 6, 1890; died December 4, 1890. Mr. Cantrell is a physician and lives at Clinton, Ill.

Martha A. Cantrell was born January 10, 1872. Married J. P. Lichtenberger June 29, 1892. They have two children: Muriel, born March 26, 1893, and Yolande, born March 19, 1898. Mr. Lichtenberger is a minister in the Christian church.

ELIZABETH CANTRELL was born May 9, 1835. Married Robert King September 21, 1855. They had three children: Alice M., Charlie and Hattie B.

Alice M. King was born July 21, 1856. Married W. S. Harrold December 30, 1886, at Leroy, Ill. Their children are: Helen L., born August 24, 1888, and Welby K., born June 5, 1891. Mr. Harrold is a farmer and lives near Wapella, Ill.

Charlie King, born August 20, 1857. Married Clara B. Hummel March 4, 1881. Their children are: L. Mae, born May 5, 1882; Pearl E., born November 24, 1885; Queenie, born October 23, 1887; Robert H., born September 15, 1890; Florence E., born December 23, 1896, and Charles W., born March 20, 1898. Mr. King is a bookkeeper, and lives in St. Louis, Mo.

Hattie B. King was born November 7, 1858. Married Abram Fry November 26, 1878. They live at Iroquois, S. D., and have two children: Robert K., born September 12, 1879, and Earle A., born July 21, 1889. Mr. Fry is a farmer.

Robert King died July 9, 1858, and his widow married William P. Shirley March 13, 1866. They had two children: Nellie and Grace.

Nellie Shirley, born May 6, 1868. Married James H. Long March 2, 1887. They live on a farm near Holdredge, Neb., and have one child, Ethel Gladys, born July 4, 1890.

Grace Shirley, born August 30, 1870. Married Hiram H. Crumbaugh December 23, 1891. They live on a farm near Leroy, Ill., and have one child, Clifford L., born July 31, 1894. Mr. Shirley died September 10, 1883. His widow lives in Leroy, Ill.

Ira J. Cantrell was born April 23, 1837. Married Martha E. Wooton December 15, 1859. She died September 23, 1860, and he married Sarah J. McLaughlin August 23, 1866. She was born April 14, 1838. Their children are: Gilbert H., Myra M., Ira J. and Cyrus D., twins, Luella and Estella, twins. There are a number of families in this record that have twins, but this is the only one that has them twice.

Gilbert H., born April 12, 1869. Married Ethol Nicholl September 30, 1896. She was born November 1, 1875. Mr. Cantrell is a traveling salesman and lives in Kansas City, Mo.

Myra M., born July 18, 1871.

Ira J., Jr., and Cyrus Duncan, twins, born Aug. 18, 1873.

Luella and Estella, twins, born September 28, 1875. Estella died October 3, 1875.

MARY CANTRELL was born July 13, 1840. Died October 30, 1875. Married Milan Harper December 17, 1863. They had four children: Edwin, born December —, 1865, died February —, 1867; Nettie G., born June —, 1867, died August —, 1868; Harriet and Joanna, twins, born November 18, 1869. Mr. Harper moved from Illinois to Fredonia, Kan., where Mrs. Harper died. He is married again and lives at Harper, Kan.

Harriet V. Harper married Arthur L. Tucker January 27, 1889. They have six children, and live on a farm near Harper, Kan.

Anna B. Harper married Martin L. Gates January 15, 1891. They live on a farm near Anthony, Kan., and have two children: Bertie V., and Jessie J. M.

MILES TROTTER CANTRELL was born November 11, 1843. Married Isabelle Akers Martin December 24, 1863. They had eight children: Corwin C., Ingham, Ann Maria, John M., Samuel T., Vida L., Harry G. and James T. Mr. Cantrell is deputy postmaster in Fredonia, Kan.

Corwin C. Cantrell was born January 25, 1866. Married Ella H. Cowgill April 11, 1888. They have two children: Fay Isabelle, born February 13, 1889, and Lida Cowgill, born January 17, 1891. Mr. Cantrell lives in Fredonia, Kan., and is a dealer in grain and coal.

Ingham Cantrell was born July 28, 1868. Died March 15, 1874.

Ann M. Cantrell was born May 28, 1871. Died September 2, 1881.

John M. Cantrell was born December 26, 1873. Died March 8, 1875.

Samuel T. Cantrell was born January 12, 1876. He is in the 'Frisco general freight office at Wichita, Kan.

Vida L. Cantrell was born May 4, 1879. Died April 8, 1880.

Harry G. Cantrell was born September 14, 1881.

James T. Cantrell was born August 13, 1884.

ALMA CANTRELL, born May 28, 1846. Died December 30, 1847.

ALMA J. CANTRELL was born November 5, 1847. Married John W. Gring November 23, 1880. They have two children: Harry C., born July 3, 1882, and Estella, born September 12, 1887. Mr. Gring is a farmer and lives near Weedman, Ill.

JOHN E. CANTRELL, born November 9, 1849. Died May 2, 1872.

ALBERT CANTRELL, born March 6, 1852. Died December 14, 1852.

EVALINE CANTRELL was born November 16, 1853. Died June 12, 1885. Married W. S. Harrold October 19, 1876. They had four children: Roy M., born April 11, 1878; Berzie A., born November 27, 1879; John L., born February 17, 1881, died September 6, 1882; and Laura B., born June 26, 1882. Mr. Harrold married Alice M. King. See her name.

MARCUS B. CANTRELL, born July 21, 1857. Died August 25, 1858.

JAMES M. CANTRELL

Was born April 10, 1810. Died April 27, 1866. Married Eliza McLaughlin August 9, 1832. She was born March 22, 1811. Died June 14, 1881. Their children are: Sarah J., born July 13, 1833, died January 24, 1857; Elmira A., born January 11, 1837; Eliza J. W., born August 30, 1847.

SARAH J. CANTRALL married James F. Duff September 14, 1852. He was born November 27, 1823. Died April 6, 1854. Their children are: Sarah Eliza, born October 2, 1853, and Elmira Jane, born September 22, 1854, died in infancy; Myra Ann and Mary Jemima, twins, born September 21, 1856.

Myra Duff married Joseph Black July 26, 1876. He died February 18, 1881. One child, Robert Lucian, born March 1879. Mr. Duff's widow married A. Catta Piatt in 1885. They have one child, Dale, born April 1, 1893.

ELMIRA A. CANTRELL married George W. Rowell October 3, 1854. Their children are: Jemima Jane, born September 22, 1858. Married Archibald S. McKee February 14, 1878. Their children are: Jennie Lutes, born December 11, 1878; Lillian, born May 19, 1884; Mary, born June 9, 1887. Mr. McKee is a dentist and lives at Vincennes, Ind.

Mrs. Rowell married Abner J. Lutes April 10, 1861. He was born May 23, 1822; died December 29, 1881. Their children are: Lillian, born Aug. 12, 1862; one son, born March 8, 1866, died in infancy.

Abner James, born April 27, 1872. He is with the U. S. Express Co. at Springfield, Ill.

Lillian married Thomas C. Harry May 14, 1884. He was born January 11, 1857. They have one child, Helene Elmira, born May 8, 1885. Mr. Harry is a lumber dealer in Atlanta, Ill.

ELIZA J. W. CANTRELL married Samuel H. Piatt June, 1869. Their child, Nita, born December 16, 1874, died December 27, 1874, and Jay Cantrell, born November 8, 1876, and Ethel, born August 3, 1884. They live in Clarron, Iowa.

SARAH CANTRELL

Was born March 14, 1812. Died November 28, 1887. Married Joshua M. Cantrell. See his name.

ZEBULON PIKE CANTRELL

Was born January 17, 1814. Died April 24, 1876. Married Elizabeth Paulk October 16, 1838. She was born January 11, 1818. Died June 12, 1852. Their children are: Amos A., William L., Martha Jane, Sarah A., Mary E. and Eliza D.

Amos A. CANTRELL was born May 11, 1840. Enlisted September 20, 1861, in Co. L, Fourth Illinois Cavalry, and was honorably discharged June 18, 1866. He lives at Cisco, Ill.

WILLIAM LEVI CANTRELL, born September 13, 1841. Died September 12, 1843.

MARTHA JANE CANTRELL, born October 3, 1842. Married Samuel G. Mott June 19, 1862. He was born June 28, 1832. Their children are: George A., born March 14, 1863; Sarah E., born November 8, 1864; Louis A., born February 4, 1867; James A., born January 11, 1869, died November 6, 1875; Clarissa E., born February 24, 1871; Joseph A., born September 10, 1873; Lillie E., born December 3, 1875, died January 24, 1876; Alonzo A., born January 3, 1877; Theodore A., born March 21, 1880, and Clarence A., born August 10, 1884.

George A. Mott married Maggie Lewis September 25, 1888. They had two children, Jessie and Waldo Emerson; both died in infancy. Mr. Mott lives at Blue Mound, Ill.

Sarah E. Mott married Marion Clark February 26, 1896. They have one child, Murvil Elmer, born November 24, 1896. They live at Oconee, Ill.

Louis A. Mott married Mary Barger January 25, 1893. She was born June 5, 1870. Died March 21, 1898. Their children are: Ina A., born March 24, 1894; Chester E., born June 10, 1895; Ethel Frances, born May 3, 1897, died January 14, 1897. Mr. Mott lives at Blue Mound, Ill.

Clarissa E. Mott married Marcus N. Cantrall. See his name.

Joseph A. Mott lives at Owaneco, Ill.

Alonzo A. Mott lives at Oconee, Ill.

Theodore A. and Clarence A. Mott live with their parents near Blue Mound, Ill.

SARAH A. CANTRELL, born December 25, 1844. Died April 30, 1872. Married Theodore A. Funk March 23, 1871. He was born December 9, 1847. They had one son; died in infancy. Mrs. Funk died, and Mr. Funk lives in Decatur, Ill.

MARY E. CANTRELL, born January 8, 1848. Married Edmund C. Hunsley January 12, 1871. He was born September 12, 1841. Their children are: Laura Agnes, born November 1, 1871; Inis Arabelle, born December 27, 1872, died September 26, 1873; John Irving, born June 30, 1874; George Howard, born April 1, 1876; Mahlon Arthur, born May 22, 1878; Charles Pike, born October 20, 1880; Mary Emily, born September 6, 1882; Frank, born March 14, 1885, died November 5, 1886; Marcellus Edmund, born July 11, 1891.

Laura A. Hunsley married Rev. R. M. Hathaway September 12, 1893. Their children are: Kenneth Adiel, born February 13, 1895, and Inez Evangeline, born July 29, 1897, died July 29, 1897. Rev. Hathaway lives near Cisco, Ill. The other children live with their parents in Cisco, Ill.

ELIZA DUNHAM CANTRELL, born December 16, 1850. Died April 9, 1851. Their mother died, and Mr. Cantrell married for a second wife Rachel Doyle November 16, 1852. Their children are: William Doyle, born October 17, 1853, died October 15, 1855; and Edgar L., born May 8, 1865. He died in infancy, and their mother died in the fall of 1865. March 14, 1872, Mr. Cantrell married Mrs. Mary Harp, whose maiden name was Everly. He died April 24, 1876, and she died January 5, 1895. Both died near Chesnut, Ill.

ELIZA CANTRELL

Was born July 4, 1816. Died January 29, 1855. Married Jeremiah P. Dunham October 5, 1834. He was born March 3, 1814. Died January 9, 1897. They had seven children: Mary Lauressa, born May 29, 1837; never married, and lives at the old home place in Waynesville, Ill.; Helen A., born June 22, 1840; Amy Letitia, born August 23, 1842; William W., born November 21, 1844; Rebecca Snow, born January 8, 1848; Eliza, born January 24, 1851; never married, and lives with her sister, Mary L.; and Jermuah P., born October 27, 1854, died August 12, 1855, with the cholera.

HELEN A. DUNHAM married George H. Whiteman February 5, 1863. Their children are: Luella, born November 25, 1865; Lena Letitia, born April 15, 1868; George Melville, born April 13, 1869; Helen Adella, born January 24, 1873.

Luella Whiteman married Joseph Whisler February 28, 1886. Their children are: Helena Pearl, born January 27,

1887; Milton J., born April 6, 1889; Della Viola, born May 27, 1895. Mr. Whisler is a barber, and lives in Tremont, Ill.

Lena L. Whiteman married George N. Bradley May 12, 1892. Their children are: J. J., born December 20, 1894, died November 18, 1896; and George Lester, born May 24, 1897. Mr. Bradley is a school teacher and lives in Minier, Ill.

George M. Whiteman married Minnie Decker December 28, 1892. Their children are: Claire Homer, born May 4, 1893, and Marguerite, born August 11, 1894. Mrs. Whitman died December 20, 1896, and Mr. Whitman lives in Minier, Ill.

Helen A. Whiteman married Robert C. Crihfield October 5, 1893. They have one child, Helen, born July 6, 1894. Mr. Crihfield is editor of the Minier News and lives in Minier, Ill.

Mrs. George Whiteman married Israel Frank April 19, 1883. He was born April 21, 1836. They have one child, Mignonette, born November 9, 1884. Mr. Frank is a brick-mason and lives in Minier, Ill.

AMY L. DUNHAM married Samuel B. Twadell October 17, 1865. He was born November 3, 1835. Died January 1, 1867. His widow married Thomas H. Ernest February 1, 1882. Their children are: Perceiville Raymond, born January 21, 1883, and Mary Esther, born September 5, 1885. They live at 322 S. Douglas avenue, Springfield, Ill.

W. W. DUNHAM married Roxanna C. Cushman March 7, 1867. She was born March 27, 1848. Died September 23, 1875. Their children are: Ivan Illa, born June 13, 1869, and Iola N., born January 3, 1873.

Ivan Illa Dunham married Fred Ball October 9, 1893. They have one child, Frederick Dunham, born March 23, 1895. Mr. Ball is attorney at law and lives in Clinton, Ill.

Mr. W. W. Dunham married for his second wife Mary J. Piercy June 13, 1878. Mr. Dunham is one of the leading merchants in Waynesville, Ill.

REBECCA S. DUNHAM married William M. Sampson July 4, 1867. He was born November 3, 1844. Their children are: Cora May, born May 5, 1869, died August 19, 1873; Leon St. Clair, born February 13, 1871, died May 9, 1871; Carrie Etna, born May 10, 1872; Mabelle, born April 15, 1875, died April 29, 1875; William Dunham, born April 28, 1876; Jennie, born January 12, 1879; Gertrude, born December 19, 1883; Lillie Maude, born July 20, 1886; Glenn Rogers, born May 6, 1889. Mr. Sampson is a merchant in Waynesville, Ill.

Carrie E. Sampson married Thurman P. Dye September 2, 1891. Their children are: Helen Fay, born March 13, 1892; infant son born February 14, 1895, died March 2, 1895; Kinneth Ross, born January 20, 1897. Mr. Dye lives at McLean, Illinois.

Jennie Sampson married J. Earl Buck March 17, 1897. They have one child, Etna Fay, born February 28, 1898. Mr. Buck lives at Waynesville, Illinois.

REBECCA CANTRELL,
(Twin to Rachel).

Were born July 25, 1818. Rebecca died March 25, 1849. Rachel died March 25, 1892.

Rebecca Cantrell married Jacob F. Sampson June —, 1836. Their children are: Carrie L., born April 4, 1842. Died August 20, 1865. She was a school teacher. Susan N., born May 6, 1844; Virginia E., born May 17, 1846; Sarah M., born March, 1848, died in infancy. Mrs. Sampson died March 24, 1849.

Susan N. Sampson married M. V. Burns October 31, 1866. Their children are: Jennie B., Nette, Frank, Fred, Caleb, Mattie G. Mr. Burns lives at Osawatomie, Kan.

Virginia E. Sampson lives in Kansas City, Mo.

RACHEL CANTRELL,
(Twin to Rebecca).

Was born April 25, 1818. Married Charles Graves October 8, 1840. He was born April 30, 1817. Left home to go to California April, 1850, and has never been heard from. They had five children; three died young; the other two are: Fanny S. and John William.

FANNY S. GRAVES was born September 11, 1841. Married Edward Storer November 2, 1858, at Wapella, Ill. They live at Burns, Kan., and have eight children: Walter N., born January 3, 1860, died August 3, 1860; Laveria, born May 9, 1861, died October 14, 1890; Lucretia E., born March 15, 1863; Joseph, born October 13, 1865, died January 21, 1884; Webster, born July 6, 1868; Howard Cantrell, born January 5, 1872; Mary Alice, born April 3, 1874, and Hattie, born September 1, 1879.

Laveria Storer married D. R. Stewart October 16, 1879. Their children are: Fannie Eliza, born August 14, 1880; Edgar, born March 16, 1883; Ethel May, born May 2, 1885, and Bessie, born June 15, 1888.

Lucretia E. Storer married D. B. Hole May 12, 1887. They have no children.

Mary A. Storer married Walter A. McIntosh February 15, 1894. They have one child, Hazlet Howard, born March 1, 1895.

Howard C. Storer married Sophia Bradley October 13, 1897.

Hattie Storer married Chester Austin December 29, 1897.

Mrs. Storer's children all live near her except Webster, who is a lawyer in Fort Worth, Tex.

JOHN WILLIAM GRAVES was born July 19, 1850. Married Martha Jane Edds March 8, 1877. She was born June 29, 1848. Their children are: Edna C., born February 8, 1878; Vella A., born September 5, 1880, died September 27, 1882; Mattie A., born January 9, 1883; Walter A., born August 10, 1885; Nina Hazel, born January 26, 1888.

WYATT CANTRELL

Was born May 11, 1821. Died January 7, 1875. Married Louisa Stephens. Died when her children were small. Their children are: ARABELLE died when a young woman, and WILLIAM H., born 1847.

WILLIAM L. CANTRELL

Was born May 15, 1823. Died June 28, 1895. Married Malinda Stout October 26, 1843. Their children are: Ann, Emeline, John K., Lydia A., Jesse, William, Sarah E. and Addie B.

ANN CANTRELL, born September 19, 1845. Married Joab Coppenbarger May 8, 1864. Their children are: William Andrew, born August 10, 1865; Laura May, born August 12, 1867; John T., born September 13, 1870, and Moses E., born September 25, 1872.

Laura M., Coppenbarger married George Whitehead September 4, 1890. He was born September 9, 1868. Their children are: Nettie M., born July 9, 1891; Roy C., born May 27, 1893; Christena, born November 8, 1897.

Moses E. Coppenbarger married Lena R. Luttrell February 15, 1893. She was born August 12, 1876. They have one child, Merna Opal, born September 7, 1894. They live at Macon City, Mo.

EMELINE CANTRELL, born October 14, 1848. Married William T. Watson September 8, 1865. Their children are: James Albert, born September 10, 1867; Nora May, born Aug. 28, 1870; William Levi, born July 26, 1872.

James A. Watson married Lina J. Ayres February 20, 1896. She was born October 12, 1871. They had one child, died in infancy, born February 12, 1897.

Nora M. Watson married Frank E. Kirby December 24, 1891. He was born December 21, 1865. They had one child, Marie, born November 5, 1892.

William L. Watson married Sylvia Johnson January 22, 1896. She was born January 13, 1876. They have one child, Clifford J., born September 20, 1897. When these children were small the mother lost her mind and was taken to the asylum, and they lived with their Grandfather Cantrell.

JOHN K. CANTRELL was born May 25, 1851. Married Mattie Burton April 2, 1876. She died, and he married Mattie Elliott, whose maiden name was Kirby, December 24, 1885.

They have one child, Elmer Lloyd, born April 12, 1890, and live at Kenney, Ill.

LYDIA A. CANTRELL, born October 14, 1853. Died October 27, 1853.

JESSE CANTRELL, born June 2, 1856. Married Adella M. Gaddis March 10, 1878. Their children are: Lulu B., born March 15, 1879. Married James A. Marlow March 3, 1898. Fred, born February 21, 1881; Louis R., born October 4, 1885; Edith M., born October 24, 1887; infant son, born April 17, 1891; died April 19, 1891; Jessie A., born April 17, 1892; Levi D., born Feb. 15, 1894, and Fern, born Nov. 14, 1897. Mr. Cantrell is a farmer and lives at Aurora, Neb.

WILLIAM CANTRELL, born September 12, 1858. Married Effa Kirby January 12, 1879. She was born October 22, 1860. Their children are: Wade Elmer, born January 10, 1881; Olive Gertrude, born June 21, 1883; Harry K., born April 16, 1889. Mr. Cantrell is a farmer and lives near Kenney, Ill.

SARAH E. (Dora) CANTRELL, born July 16, 1861. Died July 1, 1864.

ADDIE B. CANTRELL, born September 17, 1863. Married Edward E. Beam September 3, 1882. Their children are: Charlie William, born July 13, 1883; Effie Mae, born November 30, 1884; Eunice Melvina, born October 11, 1886; Earl A., born October 28, 1888; Horace Noble and Forest Levi, twins, born September 10, 1890; Earnest Cantrell, born November 14, 1892; Lula Viola, born April 2, 1895; Edna Addie, born September 8, 1897. Wm. Cantrell married for his second wife Christina Everly. After his death she married again.

JAMES CANTRELL.

Second son of Joshua, was born August 24, 1775. Died August 24, 1778.

CHRISTOPHER CANTRELL.

Third son of Joshua, was born May 16, 1778. Died without any family.

JOSHUA CANTRALL.

Fourth son of Joshua, was born April 3, 1779. Died August 11, 1840. Married Rachel McCollam April 11, 1799. She was born April 2, 1781. Died January 1, 1849. They were married in Virginia; moved to Kentucky and remained there until the uprising of the Cherokee Indians, leaving just one week before the massacre of the settlers took place. He had a flint-lock gun with which he killed over 1,000 deer. Thomas D. Cantrall, now in Fredonia, Kansas, has the gun. From Kentucky they moved to Ohio, where he engaged in farming and running a tannery. Moved to where Waynesville, Illinois, now is in 1835. His will was the first one probated in DeWitt county. His daughter, Polly, was the first to get married in DeWitt county after its organization.

They had thirteen children: Elizabeth, Jane, Thirza, Zebulon, Mahala, Polly, William, Levi, Nancy, Joshua C., Seth, Eli, Rachel.

ELIZABETH CANTRELL

Was born February 27, 1800. Died August 15, 1801.

JANE CANTRELL

Was born August 4, 1801. Died in 1860. Married Joseph W. Center November 27, 1817. Their children are: Joshua, Thirza, Elizabeth, James, Levi, Rachel, Robert, Almeda, Martha Washington.

THIRZA CENTER married Mr. Argo. ELIZABETH CENTER married Mr. Bumgarner. JAMES CENTER married Miss Burgage. RACHEL died single. ROBERT CENTER married Martha Hartwell. ALMEDA CENTER married George Sumpter. MARTHA W. CENTER married Alexandria Russel. The above is all the record I could get of the Center family.

THIRZA CANTRALL

Was born December 25, 1802. Died December 27, 1886. Married John Humphrey January 8, 1824. He was born June 15, 1797. Died November 17, 1882. Their children are: William F., Joshua C., Thomas C., Zebulon R., Milton M., Mary J., Levi A., Elizabeth E., and Rachel Annie.

WILLIAM F. HUMPHREY, born November 15, 1824. Died December 7, 1882. Married Elizabeth E. Wolf December 11, 1851. She was born January 4, 1830. Their children are: Samantha Jane, born September 12, 1852, died August 4, 1856; John William, born July 4, 1854, died January 6, 1863; Elizabeth Ellen, born October 13, 1856; Laura Ann, born February 27, 1859; Rebecca Emma, born February 23, 1862, died August 21, 1863; and Thirza Juletta, born February 25, 1864.

Elizabeth E. Humphrey married Theodore G. Edminston June 27, 1877. Their children are: William Curtis, born January 5, 1880. Lives with his Grandmother Humphrey in Clinton, Illinois. Mr. Edminston died January, 1883, and his widow died January 22, 1892.

Laura A. Humphrey married Samuel G. Creviston October 3, 1882. He was born December 22, 1856. Their children are: William, born March 16, 1884; Kate, born May 27, 1886, died November 20, 1890; Ella, born October 11, 1888; Louise, born March 30, 1891; Grace, born July 6, 1896. Mr. Creviston is a printer and works on the Lincoln Times, Lincoln, Illinois.

Thirza J. Humphrey married Harvey L. Merriman. They live in Clinton, Illinois.

JOSHUA C. HUMPHREY, born November 26, 1826. Died August 6, 1877. Married Sarah McClimans January 6, 1855. Their children are: Robert H., died in infancy, and Andrew J., born October 10, 1856; David, Charles, Nora and Rachel J.

Andrew B. Humphrey married Catherine Estel Hunter February 18, 1875. She was born February 18, 1857. Their children are: Joshua William, born May 2, 1875; Melissa La-Verne, born October 17, 1878. Married Philip M. Marvel December 29, 1897. He was born February 11, 1872. They live in Hallsville, Illinois. Mr. Humphrey's wife died September 16, 1881, and he married Sarah Jenetta Garrett July 26, 1885. She was born June 30, 1865. Their children are: Andrew Garrett, born September 5, 1888; Lewis Andrew, born December 18, 1892; Wilhemina, born October 4, 1896. Mr. Humphrey lives in Chicago, Illinois.

Charles Humphrey. He lives in Colorado Springs.

Nora Humphrey married Charles A. Downs. They live in Colorado Springs, Col.

THOMAS C. HUMPHREY, born February 22, 1828. Died September 28, 1855. Married Margaret McClimans October 22, 1854. His widow married Robert Black. They live near Midland City, Illinois.

ZEBULON R. HUMPHREY, born August 24, 1829. Died January 16, 1895. Married Margaret R. Wolf September 16, 1852. She was born May 13, 1835. Their children are: Joseph R., born August 3, 1853, died September 3, 1869; Thomas C., born April 3, 1856, died March 29, 1857; William F., born January 17, 1858, died February 19, 1873; Clara, born June 30, 1860. Married Robert M. Wildman October 26, 1880. Mr. Wildman is a railroad man and lives in Lincoln, Illinois. Their children are: Ethel, born December 23, 1881, died in infancy; Bertie L., born March 6, 1883; Margaret Ruby, born September 20, 1887; John Franklin, born December 2, 1865. Married Histery Viola Pruitt November 1, 1888. She was born March 25, 1870. Their children are: Helen Rosebrook, born December 12, 1889; Frances Lucille, born February 4, 1893. Mr. Humphrey is a minister in the M. E. church.

MILTON M. HUMPHREY, born November 8, 1832. Never married, and died July 4, 1878.

MARY J. HUMPHREY, born November 17, 1834. Died November 19, 1882. Married William Litsinberger May 20, 1856.

Their children are: Wililam married Miss Smalley. She died, and he married again. Lives at Centralia. James Albert, born August 19, 1857, died May 1, 1877. Mr. Litsinberger lives at Trinidad, Colorado.

LEVI A. HUMPHREY, born July 18, 1837. Died December 23, 1874. Married Nannie Elliott January 1, 1872. They had one child. It died when about 3 years old. His widow married again and lives in Colorado Springs, Col.

ELIZABETH E. HUMPHREY, born May 14, 1840. Died March 22, 1877. Married David McClimans March 15, 1860. He was born August 20, 1841. Their children are: Annabelle, born May 7, 1861. Married Charles D. Bowels August 22, 1881. He was born April 30, 1858. Their children are: William David, born September 5, 1882; Myra Frances, born September 2, 1884; Ella May, born October 15, 1886; Olla Bell, born March 10, 1888; Elvy Lue, born June 15, 1863, died in infancy; Laura Emma, born June 5, 1864. Married Spencer A. Samuel September 14, 1884. He was born January 7, 1860, died May 11, 1886. They had one child, Maude, born August 12, 1885. Mrs. Samuels married Arthur C. Bell December 5, 1897. He was born August 25, 1853. Mr. Bell is a carpenter and lives at Hallsville, Illinois.

Eva Jane, born May 28, 1869. Married John H. McKinney May 9, 1897. They have one child, John Carrol, born June 14, 1898. Mr. McKinny has a store in Hallsville, Illinois.

John Luther, born July 16, 1871. Lives at Monte Vista, Colo.

William Fletcher, born February 13, 1873. Is in the grocery business in Midland City, Illinois.

RACHEL ANNIE HUMPHREY, born January 19, 1844. Died August 26, 1872. Married Thomas R. Irwin November 9, 1865. They had one child, Ora Etta, born October 1, 1866. Married Charles M. Watson October 16, 1887. Their children are: Helen, born November 18, 1888; Louise, born July 15, 1891; Harry Irwin, born April 24, 1895. Mrs. Watson lives in Midland City, Illinois.

ZEBULON CANTRALL

Was born August 24, 1805. Died September 3, 1861. Married Mary (Polly) McLain March 27, 1828. She was born February 19, 1809. Died February 22, 1882. Their children are: James McLain, Rachel McCollam, Robert Andrew, Smith Minturn, Thomas Dunham, Mary Elizabeth, Charles Roger.

JAMES M. CANTRELL was born March 14, 1830. Died November 28, 1868. Married Amanda M. Lanterman September 15, 1855. She was born September 9, 1834. Their children are: Mary Elizabeth, Smith, Larue, Franklin. Mrs. Cantrall married Robert Cantrall February 9, 1875. They live at Norwood, Illinois.

Mary E. Cantrall married W. Graham. They had eleven children. Five died in infancy. The other six are: Grace, Stella, Winnie, Roy Larue, Jessie L., Gertrude. They live at Cresson, Texas. Smith L. Cantrell died April 9, 1894. His widow and three children live at Frazier, Oklahoma Territory.

Franklin Cantrall was born September 12, 1864. Died November 15, 1864.

RACHEL M. CANTRELL was born August 8, 1834. Died August 10, 1860. Married Henry C. Haughey October 7, 1856. Their children are: Mary, died; R. Minnie, born July 20, 1860, died September 20, 1863.

ROBERT A. CANTRALL was born October 23, 1836. Died September 13, 1845.

SMITH M. CANTRALL was born August 28, 1839. Married Hannah O. Williams August 6, 1863. They have several children and live in Waconda, South Dakota.

THOMAS D. CANTRALL was born March 27, 1841. Married H. Alma Fox September 22, 1863. Their children are: Frank Ross, Charles McKee, Robert Fox, Jessie McLain.

Frank R. Cantrall was born November 30, 1865. Married Mary D. G. Lansdon December 24, 1891.

Charles M. Cantrell, born August 4, 1869. Married Anna Hawley Wood June 28, 1893. She was born October 25, 1870. Their children are: Thomas Harvey, born August 20, 1894, died in infancy; Archibald Martin, born August 30, 1896. Mr. Cantrall is a minister in the Presbyterian church.

Robert F. Cantrall, born January 28, 1874. Married M. Etta Stroud November 26, 1896. They have one child, Thomas E., born August 17, 1897.

Jessie M. Cantrall, born September 23, 1877. Married Oliver C. Wilson December 18, 1895. They have one child, Horace Wilson, born September 15, 1897. Mr. Cantrall lives on a farm near Fredonia, Kansas.

MARY E. CANTRALL was born June 30, 1845. Died March 1, 1848.

CHARLES R. CANTRALL was born June 9, 1853. Married Alice McCrary December 17, 1873. Their children are: Carrie Fern, born August 25, 1875; Frank D., born July 14, 1880; Walter C., born January 22, 1883; Nettie Fay, born April 8, 1889. Mr. Cantrall is in the real estate and insurance business in Fredonia, Kansas.

MAHALA CANTRALL

Was born July 1, 1807. Died September 17, 1857. Married Elijah Hull March 12, 1835. He was born April 13, 1812. Died April 25, 1884. Their children are: Levi C., Joshua C., Sarah Ann, Martha Emeline, Thomas W., Josiah Porter.

LEVI C. HULL, born June 24, 1836. Married Maggie Adams in 1858. Their children are: Nellie, Robert, Newel, John, Kate. Mr. Hull lives at Stark, Fla.

JOSHUA C. HULL, born November 3, 1838. Married Adeline Harrold February 5, 1863. She was born June 23, 1844. Their children are: Minnie A., Sherman G., Edna V., Anna J., Emmett K.

Minnie A. Hull, born August 5, 1865. Married C. W. Samuel December 25, 1884. He was born August 27, 1861. Their children are: Harry Earl, born December 4, 1886, died January 22, 1887; Nellie Blanche, born May 26, 1888. They live on a farm one mile west of Wapella, Illinois.

Sherman G. Hull, born March 6, 1867. Married Leona May Harrison March 8, 1894. They have one child, Cecil B., born February 28, 1895. Mr. Hull is a druggist in Clinton, Illinois.

Edna V. Hull, born October 3, 1869. Married Charles C. Duzan December 30, 1896. They live with her father.

Anna J. Hull, born August 1, 1876. Married Luther M. Argo February 3, 1897. They live near Wapella, Illinois.

Emmett K. Hull, born March 28, 1887. Herbert Hughes Hull, son of Josiah P. Hull, has lived at Joshua C.'s since a small child. Mr. Hull, since the war, has lived on his farm, three miles west of Wapella, Illinois.

SARAH ANN HULL, born December 14, 1841. Died January 22, 1892. Married James Longbrake January 23, 1866. He was born January 21, 1843. Their children are: Emma Nettie, Claude Franz, Mahala (May) E., and Lemoine, Harrold, Percy, Willard Dean, Elijah Hull and Jennie Esther.

Emma N. Longbrake, born October 26, 1866. Married Albert T. McKee February 20, 1889. He was born June 6, 1864. Their children are: Grace Elma, born March 9, 1890; Alta Verneal, born June 28, 1893. Mr. McKee works at the Illinois Central machine shops, Clinton, Illinois.

Claude F. Longbrake, born September 10, 1868. Married Della Swisher October 18, 1893. She was born September 2, 1868. Mr. Longbrake is a painter at I. C. shops, Clinton, Illinois.

Mahala E. Longbrake, born February 23, 1871. Married Clayton Letchner May 24, 1892. Their children are: Paul, born May 26, 1893, died September 15, 1894; Claude Myron, born February 13, 1895, and Mahlon, born October 23, 1896. They live on a farm near Wapella, Ill.

Lemoine H. Longbrake, born May 21, 1872. Lives at Wapella, Illinois.

Percy Longbrake, born April 9, 1874, died in infancy.

Willard D. Longbrake, born July 18, 1875. Lives with his father near DeWitt, Illinois.

Elijah H. Longbrake, born March 22, 1878. He is a school teacher at Parnell, Illinois.

Jennie E. Longbrake, born December 19, 1883. Is at home with her father near DeWitt, Illinois.

MARTHA EMELINE HULL, born January 13, 1843. Married J. L. Longbrake February 19, 1863. Their children are: Jessie L., born February 9, 1865, died February 17, 1886; Marquis N., born June 17, 1867; Lloyd, born November 29, 1869; Guy A. born March 28, 1872; Meta, born March 17, 1874, died March 18, 1874; George R., born May 9, 1875; Delbert L., born September 2, 1878, died Sept. 13, 1879; Bertha E., born November 19, 1880, died November 9, 1892. Their home is at Galesburg, Illinois.

Guy A. Longbrake is a practicing physician at Galesburg, Illinois.

THOMAS W. HULL, born January 1, 1846. Married Maggie A. Adams February 6, 1872. They had one son, Elijah A., born December 2, 1872. Mrs. Hull died and he married Alice Jones and lives at Stockville, Neb.

JOSIAH P. HULL married Sadie Argo Hughes. They had one child, Herbert H., born July 5, 1877, and lives with his uncle, Joshua Hull. Mrs. Hull died July 7, 1877, and Mr. Hull married Sophia Welsh. They have three children: Fay, Jennie and Opal. Their home is at Phillips, Neb.

POLLY CANTRALL

Was born February 8, 1810. Died May 10, 1872. Married William H. Jones May 21, 1839. He was born January 18, 1812, died February 3, 1872. Their children are: Hester Ann, Lucinda Moore, James T., Rachel E., Nancy J., William H., Mary Ellen.

HESTER A. JONES, born September 16, 1840. Married James A. Ball December 4, 1860. Their child, Olive, married John M. Jackson October 5, 1882. One daughter, Minnie Olive, was born to them, and Mrs. Jackson died April 21, 1886. Marion died in infancy. Walter I. is married and lives in Wyoming. Robert A. is married and is a minister in the M. E. church in Nebraska. Taliday R. is married; lives in Texas; is a railroad agent and has lost one of his arms. Dessie Polly is married, has two children, and lives in Emporia, Kansas. Hester E. is married and lives in Nebraska. Charles E. is married, and is a school teacher in Nebraska. Perry J., James Garfield and Lucy are at home at Hamingford, Neb.

LUCINDA M. JONES, born January 15, 1842. Married W. F. Herman July 4, 1871. They live on a farm, three miles west of Wapella, Illinois.

JAMES T. JONES, born October 28, 1843. Married Mary Harrold. Their children are: Lillie, Clarence, Edith. They live at Burlington, Col.

RACHEL E. JONES, born September 29, 1845. Married John A. Smith December 13, 1866. He was born April 6, 1843. Their children are: Welbey Euphena, born October 4, 1867, died in infancy; Edgar, born May 4, 1869, is at home; Maurice Ozro, born April 2, 1871; Claude, born February 25, 1873; Estella, born July 6, 1876; Elsie Maude, born June 5, 1879, is at home; Ina May, born May 27, 1886, died September 1, 1887.

Maurice O. Smith married Lettie DeVault June 22, 1892. Their child, Francis Maurice, born March 27, 1894. They live in Springfield, Illinois.

Claude Smith married Lulu Johnson March 31, 1896. They live in Springfield, Illinois.

Estella Smith married Norman Fortune May 25, 1898. Mr. Smith served four years on the war and lives in Springfield, Illinois.

NANCY J. JONES, born December 20, 1846. Died October 23, 1847.

WILLIAM H. JONES, born May 24, 1848. Never married. Is a blacksmith at Midland City, Illinois.

MARY E. JONES, born July 21, 1853. Died December 16, 1884.

WILLIAM CANTRALL

Was born April 1, 1812. Died December 15, 1886. Married Nancy McClure November 27, 1834. She was born July 27, 1810. Died September 13, 1874. Their children are: Henry M., Rachel P., Margaret, William H.

HENRY M. CANTRALL died in infancy.

RACHEL P. CANTRALL, born December 5, 1838. Married William Metzger November 13, 1855. He was born February 9, 1826. Their children are: Minnie B., born October 24, 1858, died January 8, 1867; Harry M., born May 14, 1868. Married Katie Beammont October 28, 1895. They live in Grand Rapids, Mich. William Metzger lives in Clinton, Illinois.

MARGARET CANTRALL died in infancy.

WILLIAM H. CANTRALL was born December 27, 1843. Married Deborah Earsom March 8, 1864. She was born December 9, 1841. Their children are: Johnny, born January 3, 1865, died February 17, 1865; George M., born July 20, 1866. Married Lizzie Klaas January 28, 1896. They have one child, Lawrence William Henry, born January 13, 1897. Their home is Galesburg, Illinois; and Harry, born August 29, 1871, married Mrs. Frances Luella Snow, whose maiden name was Lawrence, January 27, 1898. They live with his parents, whose home is one mile south of Waynesville, Illinois.

LEVI CANTRALL

Was born May 6, 1814. Married Elizabeth G. Robb October 17, 1839. She was born December 14, 1815. Their children are: LOUISA JANE, born October 27, 1840, died April 15, 1896. She never married and lived with her parents; JOHN R. CANTRALL was born January 21, 1842. Married Jennie Love October 6, 1870. She was born July 4, 1845. Their children are: Alva L., born August 2, 1871, lives with his parents and is in the real estate and loan business with his father at Tuscola, Illinois; Edna E., born March 11, 1873, graduated in a training school for nurses in St. Louis, Mo., in 1896, and since then has practiced in St. Louis. She is the second trained nurse that I have learned of in the tribe; Myrta Maud, born December 12, 1879, died November 8, 1897. The last child of Levi was NANCY ANN, born April 29, 1844, died March 15, 1875. She lived at home, never married and was an invalid most of her life.

NANCY CANTRALL

Was born June 13, 1816. Died December 15, 1894. Married James R. Robb March 26, 1840. He was born July 26, 1814. Died November 16, 1847. Their children are: Joshua C., Francis Marion, Hugh.

JOSHUA C. ROBB was born March 21, 1841. Took sick in the army, came home and died April 28, 1862.

FRANCIS MARION ROBB, born Nov. 19, 1842. Died March 1886. Married Elvira Bridges September 18, 1866. They have one daughter, Maude A., born July 18, 1867. Married E. H. McFarland. They have one child, James, born October, 1897. They live in Chicago. Mrs. Robb lives with her daughter.

Hugh Robb, born September 3, 1846. Married Josie S. Scroggy February 26, 1880. She was born November 29, 1853. Their children are: H. Earl, born December 5, 1881, died November 25, 1887; James Humphrey Lenierb, born January 30, 1886. Mr. Robb is a druggist in Heyworth, Ill.

JOSHUA C. CANTRALL.

Was born September 20, 1818. Died March 31, 1897. Married Mary Jane Robb April 29, 1841. She was born May 30, 1823. Died September 20, 1855. Their children are: Nancy Jane, James, Martha Ann, Rachel, and a son born September 18, 1855, died in infancy.

NANCY JANE CANTRALL was born April 17, 1842. Died September 12, 1844.

JAMES CANTRALL was born June 19, 1845. Married Mary J. Lanham November 24, 1870. She was born January 10, 1843, Died March 30, 1889. Their children are: Farrel, born January 16, 1872, died October 7, 1872; Earnest, born July 16, 1874, died September 28, 1874; Nellie M., born August 8, 1875; Mabel C., born March 12, 1879. Mr. Cantrall married Mrs. Christianna H. Stewart, whose maiden name was Huckleberry, November 28, 1889. She was born February 24, 1846. They live at Waynesville, Ill.

MARTHA ANN CANTRALL was born April 11, 1847. Died July 19, 1849.

RACHEL CANTRALL was born December 13, 1850. Married Alva C. Ingham March 21, 1872. They live on a farm near Warrensburg, Ill., and have three children: George Paul, born March 16, 1875; Mabel Claire, born May 19, 1877, and Anna Mary, born June 3, 1881.

Joshua C. Cantrall married Margaret M. Leeper March 4, 1856. She was born May 28, 1822. Died October 1, 1893.

SETH CANTRALL

Was born August 25, 1821. Died August 7, 1824.

ELI CANTRALL

Was born February 6, 1824. Died June 17, 1876. Married Zurilda Robb, whose maiden name was Lanterman, December 5, 1854. Died December 11, 1874. They had two children: Annie Laurie and Sophia.

ANNIE L. CANTRALL married William Tracy. They have several children. Mr. Tracy is a blacksmith.

SOPHIA CANTRALL married Cornelius Cunningham. Mr. Cunningham is a barber.

RACHEL CANTRALL

Was born April 23, 1826. Died July 24, 1829.

THOMAS CARSEY CANTRALL.

Fifth son of Joshua, was born October 11, 1782. Died September 30, 1797.

WILLIAM G. CANTRALL.

The sixth son of Joshua, was born September 6, 1784. Died March 6, 1867. Married Deborah Mitts in 1804. She was born November 16, 1785. Died March 15, 1856. They had twelve children: Dorothy, Ann, Elizabeth, Joshua M., Thirza, Adam M., Deborah, Mahala, Susannah, William M., Maranda and Andrew Jackson.

DOROTHY CANTRALL

Was born March 15, 1805. Died August 11, 1855. Married Charles Snelson. They moved to Iowa and raised a large family, where they died, but I have been unable to get their record.

ANN CANTRALL

Was born August 1, 1806. Died December 25, 1855. Married John W. Snelson. They moved to Iowa, raised a large family, and died there, but I have failed in getting a record of the family.

ELIZABETH CANTRALL

Was born August 29, 1808. Died July 15, 1878. Married Joseph D. Langston July 23, 1829. He was born December 25, 1805. Their children are: William C., born April 25, 1830; Emily, born in 1832, died May 8, 1872; Theresa and John, twins, born May 11, 1834. She died June 22, 1856, and he was killed in the army December 15, 1864, (see below); and James B., born November 29, 1836.

WILLIAM C. LANGSTON married Elizabeth J. Fagan October 28, 1851. She died December 26, 1853, and he married Eliza J. King June 17, 1855. There were no children.

EMILY LANGSTON married Asaph Bates. She died May 8, 1872. Their children are: Theresa E., John T., Elizabeth A., Emily S. and Joseph W. Live in Kansas.

JOHN LANGSTON married Martha Price April 11, 1862. They had one child, Eva Jane. Mr. Langston enlisted in August, 1862, in Co. C, 114th Illinois Infantry, and was killed at the battle of Nashville, Tenn., December 15, 1864.

JAMES B. LANGSTON married Eliza Taylor. Their children are: Sarah A., Mary A., John O., Ida L. and Beulah.

JOSHUA M. CANTRALL

Was born December 17, 1810. Died January 18, 1881. Married Sarah Cantrell January 14, 1834. She was born March 14, 1812. Died November 28, 1887. Their children are: Zebulon G., William G., Matilda, Isaac, Jacob M., Joshua G., Mahala E., Sarah, John A. and George A.

ZEBULON G. CANTRALL was born May 7, 1835. Died May 3, 1896. Married Elizabeth J. Lilly November 6, 1864. She was born November 19, 1838. Their children are: Mary A., born March 1, 1866, died September 11, 1889; Melissa E., born October 31, 1867. Married William S. Womack October 15, 1890. He was born October 14, 1870. They have no children and live in Springfield, Ill. Celia J., born December 18, 1869. Married Frank A. Gillman October 18, 1887. He was born November 13, 1869. They have three children: Harry Alvin, born January 18, 1888; Mabel Lilly, born April 25, 1890; Blanche Celia, born July 2, 1892. Mr. Gillman is an artist. Lives in Indianapolis, Ind.

Noah M., born September 4, 1871. Died November 9, 1893; Arminta L. and Amelia F., twins, were born August 23, 1873; Arminta died October 20, 1891, and Amelia died November 24, 1879; Alfred E., born December 17, 1875, and Zebulon G., born July 8, 1878. Alfred and Zebulon live with their mother in Springfield, Ill.

WILLIAM G. CANTRALL was born February 20, 1837. Married Mary Jane Randall January 5, 1862. She was born January 26, 1839. Their children are: Marcus Newton, born November 10, 1862; Sarah Matilda, born February 9, 1863; Mary Laurissa, born September 11, 1865; Louisa Mahala, born June 19, 1867; Deborah Anna, born December 1, 1868, died March 8, 1869; Rebecca Frances, born January 6, 1870; John William, born June 12, 1871; Ida Narcissus, born August 29, 1874, died September 11, 1874; Wilbur Franklin, born November 20, 1875.

Marcus N. married Sarah J. Saunders February 16, 1889. She died September 26, 1894, and Mr. Cantrall married Effie C. Mott November 7, 1895. They have one child, Maud Jane, born November 4, 1897. Their home is at Blue Mound, Ill.

Sarah M. Cantrall married Henry B. Mallory May 27, 1896. They have one child, John W., born July 30, 1897. Their home is at Pilot, Ill.

Mary L. Cantrall married Herman Miller October 24, 1894. They have one child. They live near Cantrall, Ill.

Louisa M. Cantrall married John E. Strode December 24, 1890. Their children are: Jacob E., born March 4, 1892; Everett E., born September, 1893, died September 27, 1894; Harry J., born January 4, 1895; Mary J., born December 2, 1896. They live near Cantrall, Ill.

MATILDA CANTRALL was born September 15, 1838. Died August 31, 1839.

ISAAC CANTRALL was born February 7, 1840. Died September 4, 1844.

JACOB M. CANTRALL was born December 26, 1841. Married Marion J. Tufts December 22, 1869. She was born May 14, 1848. Died March 26, 1879. Their children are: Lucretia and Sarah, twins, died in infancy; Addie E. and Cora M.

Addie E. Cantrall was born February 7, 1873. Married Edward Morgret March 25, 1890. Their children are: Roy Ray and Floy May, twins, born May 17, 1898. They live on a farm near Stonington, Ill.

Cora M. Cantrall, born October 12, 1878. Married James M. Alexander February 9, 1898. He was born March 1, 1875. They live with her father. January 15, 1880, Mr. Cantrall married Martha Brown. She was born August 28, 1862. Died January 16, 1898. Their children are: Earnest Jacob, born

July 15, 1883, and Ula Joshua, born June 4, 1886. They live near Cantrall, Ill.

JOSHUA G. CANTRALL, born May 28, 1843. Died December 12, 1847.

MAHALA E. CANTRALL, born October 4, 1845. Died March 16, 1887. Married George W. Bailey October 9, 1873, being his second wife. He was born March 12, 1825. Mr. Bailey was a soldier in the Mexican war and for one year was Captain of Co. H, 114th Illinois Infantry. They had one child, Sarah E. born August 12, 1875. Married Earl Green. They had one child, Roy, and she married Dave Sherman. They live in Athens, Ill.

SARAH CANTRALL, born February 26, 1848. Died November 13, 1849.

JOHN A. CANTRALL, born June 10, 1850. Died October 5, 1857.

GEORGE A. CANTRALL, born October 5, 1852. Died September 23, 1857.

THIRZA CANTRALL, born November 8, 1812. She died October 7, 1851, three months after marriage. Married Edward Guyott.

ADAM M. CANTRALL, born February 27, 1815. Died January 15, 1882. Married Deliah Smith. She was born July 6, 1820. Their children are: Harriet, Jane, Hiram P., John D., Jeremiah S., Elizabeth, Martha, Eli, Charles.

HARRIET CANTRALL married William Brisentine and moved to Texas. They had one child, William Lewis, born Oct. 17, 1857. His mother died, and he came to Illinois when 5 years old. Grew to manhood in the home of Joshua M. Cantrall. Married Mary Catherine Yocum April 21, 1880. She was born June 30, 1862. Their children are: Maggie Harriet, born March 12, 1881; Anna May, born February 11, 1883; Mamie, born October 1, 1886. Their home is in Springfield, Ill.

JANE CANTRALL, born November 28, 1840. Married Theopholis Rubly September 17, 1860. He died February 23,

1876. Their children are: Mary J., born March 13, 1861; Charles, born July 15, 1867, died in infancy; Robert F., born May 22, 1870; Leslie J., born September 17, 1875. Married Polly Wilkinson December 20, 1897. She was born November 19, 1877. They live at Riverton, Ill.

Robert Rubly married Eva Gaddis, and lives in Riverton, Ill.

Mrs. Jane Rubly married John Hisler January 18, 1884, and lives in Riverton.

Hiram P. Cantrall, born November 1, 1842. Married Elizabeth Eunice. Their children are: John B., Maggie, Lottie, Nora, Lulu. Mr. Cantrall is a farmer near Paris, Ill.

John D. Cantrall was born January 6, 1844. Died September 7, 1863.

Jeremiah S. Cantrall was born November 12, 1848. Married Etta Drone. Their children are: Albert D., Annie, Willie and Wilbur, twins, died in infancy; Fanny, Oscar, Harry, Nettie. They live in Peoria, Ill.

Elizabeth Cantrall was born September 6, 1851. Married Joseph H. Hendricks January 7, 1869. He was born October 14, 1846. Their children are: Irene, born November 2, 1870; Leonard, born January 2, 1873; Parley, born September 7, 1876; Zella May, born September 17, 1880; Charles Francis, born July 9, 1883; Earl Chester, born October 29, 1885. The last four all died in infancy; Leslie, born December 30, 1887; Lilliam, born July 4, 1895. Mr. Hendricks lives in Riverton, Ill.

Martha Cantrall, born January 9, 1857. Married Richard Plunkett January 1, 1880. Their children are: Lonella, born October 26, 1875. Married Frank Crum; John Franklin, born November 2, 1880, and one died in infancy. They live in Illiopolis, Ill.

Eli Cantrall, born March 25, 1859. Married Laura E. Barnes January 27, 1881. She was born January 13, 1863. Their children are: George H., born November 11, 1882; Minnie, born December 5, 1884; Mary Elizabeth, born January 17, 1888; John D., born April 4, 1890; Maud N., born September 4, 1892, and Verny Eli, born August 10, 1894. Mr. Cantrall is a machinist and lives at Riverton, Ill. Has run a machine in paper mill for more than 25 years.

CHARLES CANTRALL, born March 7, 1861. Married Ettie Freeman. Mr. Cantrall is a railroad and bridge carpenter.

DEBORAH CANTRELL

Was born February 16, 1817. Died June 10, 1891. Married Marshall S. Randall January 5, 1837. He was born January 26, 1831. Died September 15, 1883. Their children are: John W., Mary Jane, William H., Garrett D., Elizabeth, Louisa, Rachel, Nancy, Louis T., Deborah, Walter S., and Isaac Newton.

JOHN W. RANDALL was born November 28, 1837. Married Emily Campbell. They had one child, died in infancy. Mr. Randall is a farmer and lives at Iuka, Ill.

MARY J. RANDALL, born January 26, 1839. Married William G. Cantrall. See his name.

WILLIAM H. RANDALL, born October 31, 1840. Married Amanda McDaniel April 26, 1862. Their children are: Lulu, Dubley. Mr. Randall is an insurance agent and lives at St. Louis, Mo. His wife died and he married Annie Skyler.

GARRETT D. RANDALL, born February 25, 1842. Married Rachel Campbell. Both are dead. Their children are: Marshall S., John. Lives with his uncle, John Randall, and one died in infancy.

ELIZABETH RANDALL, born August 12, 1843. Married Abraham Morgrett. Their children are: Alice Bell, Edward, Clarissa, Mary, Ivy, Leota and Birdy. They live at Stonington, Ill.

LOUISA RANDALL, born September 16, 1845. Married German A. Ball December 16, 1869. They had one child, Silas. He is married and lives in Centralia, Ill. Mr. Randall lives in Centralia, Ill.

RACHEL RANDALL, born July 26, 1848. Married Varnum Aylesworth November 23, 1873. Their children are: Frank, John, Sarah. Mr. Aylesworth died and his widow lives at Red Willow county, Danburry, Neb.

NANCY RANDALL, born November 16, 1859. Married Lewis Upton January 1, 1876. They had one child, Arley, and Mr. Upton died. His widow lives at Danburry, Neb.

LOUIS T. RANDALL, born March 14, 1852. Married Mary Brewer June 25, 1876. She was born February 1, 1854. Their children are: William G., born April 16, 1877; Silas W., born February 3, 1880, died November 21, 1894, and Annie Pearl, born October 11, 1878, died May 1, 1879. Mr. Randall lives in Blue Mound, Ill.

DEBORAH RANDALL, born April 3, 1854. Married Aaron Brewer. They have one child, Limon, and Mr. Randall is a farmer and lives near Blue Mound, Ill.

WALTER S. RANDALL, born March 20, 1857. Married Mary Vandarian. Their children are: Rufus, Cloyd and Merble. Mr. Randall lives on a farm near Blue Mound, Ill.

ISAAC NEWTON RANDALL, born March 16, 1859. Married Lina Winters. Their children are: Mabel, Bertha, Earle, and Marvin. Mr. Randall lives on a farm near Blue Mound, Ill.

MAHALA CANTRALL

Was born December 4, 1818. Married Newton Street. He was her fourth husband, and she died, leaving no children.

SUSANNA CANTRALL

Was born November 23, 1820. Died May 12, 1863. Married Leonard Mitts. Their children are: Harrison, Jessie, Jacob, Mahala, Martha. Mr. Mitts lives near Cora Station, Sangamon county, Ill.

WILLIAM M. CANTRALL

Was born December 28, 1822. Married Adaline Claywell April 3, 1845. Their children are: Andrew J., Julia A., Miranda, James M., Peney, William J., Deborah J., Lewis E. and Sarah E.

ANDREW J. CANTRALL, born February 12, 1846. Died September 28, 1849.

JULIA A. CANTRALL, born November 28, 1847. Married Leander L. Jones September 5, 1868. Their children are: Enoch E., born August 17, 1869, died February 4, 1880; Ada A., born December 4, 1871. Married Fred W. Lewis July 1, 1891. Their children are: Lee C., born April 4, 1892, and Ray F., born April 1, 1897. Live at Jetmore, Kan. Perry A., born January 23, 1873. Married to Mary L. Dorey July 1, 1897. Florence E., born March 21, 1875, died July 22, 1876; Grace J., born February 11, 1882; Virgie A., born November 16, 1883; Ross N., born July 24, 1887; Ina H., born February 27, 1889. They live at Cleveland, O. T.

MIRANDA CANTRALL, born December 12, 1849. Died November 25, 1881. Married Roland V. Mallory September 10, 1871. Their children are: William, born June 14, 1872. Married Ida Hill January 9, 1897. They live at Decatur, Ill. Lula N., born September 20, 1874. Married Frank Whitmer March 9, 1896. They live at Decatur, Ill. Mrs. Mallory died and Mr. Mallory married again and lives at Decatur, Ill.

JAMES M. CANTRALL, born September 24, 1851. Married Catherine Long August 31, 1882. Their children are: William Arthur, born June 13, 1883; James Edward, born October 18, 1884; Johnnie Albert, born January 7, 1886; Anna May, born February 17, 1889; Ina Bell, born January 28, 1896. They live in Athens, Ill.

PERCY CANTRALL, born October 26, 1853. Married Richmond E. Whaley August 23, 1877. Their children are: Nellie F., born July 3, 1878, died in infancy; Hattie E., born January 27, 1880; William E., born April 15, 1881; Lottie F., born December 6, 1882, died February 20, 1887. Live at Noble, Kan.

WILLIAM J. CANTRALL, born September 9, 1855. Died March 20, 1862.

Deborah J. Cantrall, born August 24, 1857. Married John M. Long August 18, 1880. Their children are: William E., born June 18, 1881; Milton H., born January 4, 1883; Stella G., born January 6, 1886; Sarah A., born November 30, 1888, died in infancy; Urania, born September 27, 1890; Ancil R., born May 5, 1892; Alvin N., born September 15, 1897. Live at Noble, Kan.

LEWIS E. CANTRALL, born July 18, 1859. Married Anna Black August 26, 1882. Their children are: Nellie E., born August 13, 1883; Lucy N., born March 17, 1885. They moved from Illinois to Missouri, where Mr. Cantrall died August 1, 1885. His widow returned to Illinois and married William Mellinger. See his name.

SARAH E. CANTRALL, born November 8, 1862. She is a deaf mute and was educated at Jacksonville, Ill. Married William Trotter November 8, 1882. He is also a deaf man. Their children are: Lillie G., born December 3, 1883; Frank W., born October 4, 1885, and Jeff, born January 23, 1894. Live in Indian Territory.

William M. Cantrall enlisted in Co. C, 114th Illinois Infantry, served three years and re-enlisted and died in the hospital at Memphis, Tenn., July 8, 1864.

MIRANDA CANTRALL

Was born May 12, 1826. Married William C. Snelson July 17, 1852. He was born July 13, 1830. Died March 9, 1853. They had one child, Charles H., born April 17, 1853.

CHARLES H. SNELSON married Julia E. Saunders March 5, 1879. She was born June 6, 1857. Their children are: John W., born December 10, 1879; Addie L., born February 17, 1881; George W., born May 14, 1883; and Eliza P., born April 17, 1885.

Julia Snelson died October 7, 1885, and Mr. Snelson married Mount E. Jones November 17, 1891. She was born January 18, 1860. Their children are: Chester H., born February 11, 1892; Clara E., born August 14, 1894; Adolph C., born December 19, 1896. They live near Cantrall, Ill.

William Snelson died March 9, 1853, and his widow married Samuel Mellinger March 4, 1858. He was born January 27, 1832. There children are: William C., Mahala A., Deborah A., and Lucy E.

WILLIAM C. MELLINGER was born December 8, 1858. Married Sarah J. Wiggins April 15, 1880. She was born November 13, 1861. Their children are: Idella, born October 5, 1880; Clarence, born January 17, 1883; Anna, born August 29, 1885, and Florence, born August 21, 1887. Mrs. Mellinger died August 25, 1888, and Mr. Mellinger married Anna L. Cantrall February 19, 1890. Her maiden name was Black. They had one child, Sherman, born December 14, 1890. They live near Cantrall, Ill.

MAHALA A. MELLINGER was born November 20, 1860. Married Adolph Nelson February 25, 1885. He was born March 11, 1857. Their children are: Charles O., born March 10, 1886, died August 19, 1886; Clara E., born May 28, 1887; Stella M., born November 15, 1888; Hattie A., born September 16, 1890; Mary E., born November 29, 1891; Miranda, born August 11, 1893, died October 26, 1893; John W., born January 19, 1896. Live near Riverton, Ill.

DEBORAH A. MELLINGER was born November 12, 1862. Married James Jennings August 29, 1895. He was born December 28, 1866. Lives north of Fancy Prairie, Ill.

LUCY E. MELLINGER, born November 14, 1866, and lives with her parents.

Samuel Mellinger enlisted August 12, 1862 in Co. C, 114th Illinois Infantry for three years, served the full time and was honorably discharged August 3, 1865. He lives near Cantrall, Ill.

ANDREW JACKSON CANTRALL

Was born January 4, 1829. Died March 15, 1842.

LEVI CANTRALL.

The seventh son of Joshua, was born October 1, 1787, in Virginia. His parents moved to Kentucky in 1789. He was there married to Fanny England November 30, 1809. She was born October 2, 1792. They moved to Ohio, then to Illinois, reaching the place where Springfield now stands December 4, 1819. They journeyed north to a place near where the town of Cantrall now is, and there improved a farm where Mr. Cantrall lived until his death. The following notes are taken from writing left by him:

Events that happened since December, 1819:

December 4 I camped where Springfield now is a city. December 5 came across the Sangamon river and on the 7th looked for the location I now live on. December 8 set to build a cabin and got one raised and chinked and chimney up to the mantle, and the weather set in so hard that mortar could not be used. December 24 the snow began to fall, one snow after another, until it was two feet on a level and became extremely cold until the 11th of February. On the night of the 11th it moderated and rained until 12 o'clock. At this date there was Wyatt Cantrall, Matthew Holland, Alexander Crawford, Henry Crawford, Kellogg, John Dixon and myself, on the way to the American bottom for provisions. In the evening changed severely cold. Camped at Hickory Point. Met William Proctor with a lot of stock hogs, and 12th camped together. December 13th camped at Dory Fork. By this time our company numbered 10 men and seven teams. December 14 camped at Padies on Kohoky Creek. December 15 to the American bottom to the six mile prairie, then loaded up with meal and flour. On the 18th started home with 14 head of hogs, and the weather was thawing in the day and freezing at night and the waters began to rise and got so we had to head some streams. Some days we had to break the ice so as to let the hogs get through the sloughs. At night was cold. We come to old Father Bans, who was stuck in a snow drift for three days with a load of corn. He was badly frost bitten. We helped him out and kept him in company with us till we got to Brush Creek. There we cut him a good supply of wood for fire. The water was so high that he was to stay until the water fell, but after we left, the old man ventured in and lost a part of his corn. He was a cripple with the freezing of his feet all summer.

The next day we got seven miles to Sugar Creek. There we had to cut timber and build a bridge on the ice and drove our hogs on the ice and swim out on the land. We got over and camped. Traveled one mile that day. Next day got to where the steam distillery stands, (where the C. & A. now crosses Sangamon, north of Springfield), and camped. By this time the river got over the banks and no ferry boat or canoe we got a grubbing hoe and our ax and made a trough, and Bro. Wyatt came across to get tools to build a canoe, but did not return for days.

Fourth day while I was in camp Stephen England come with a family to the camp, and we sent a boy to Mr. Kelly's, where the city of Springfield now is, for a set of tools and made a canoe and commenced swimming and ferrying with the canoe, and on the twenty-first day from the start we and party arrived in good health and spirits.

The snow yet remained in drifts until the 10th of March. The spring was fine and we began to improve. On the 25th day of April there was a heavy rain and that was the last till the 19th of July. The drought set in and the late planted corn never came up until the July rain, and in May, the 26th, there was a frost that cut the corn to the ground.

The season was so bad that we thought about moving back to the settlement, but in August went down to the American bottom and got a load of corn, and Bro. Wyatt and as far as where Selly mill stands, and my team stuck fast in the mud. There I had to unload the corn and reload one of the hottest days in August. All the drink was out of a horse track while I was doing this. Bro. Wyatt was gone across to Spring Creek to Elias mill to get grinding. In a few days I went down to the Ridge Prairie and bought a set of mill stones and built what we then called a band mill, constructed by a large wheel 40 feet over and a rawhide or a tug around a wheel, and ground the first grain ever on the north side of the Sangamon river in the fall of 1820. Then the people came to my mill for thirty miles and in 1822, in the spring, I built a water mill. That was the only chance for the north for fifty miles for a while.

In the fall of 1830 I built a saw mill. The season was very dry, so that I could not grind none and had my hands to dig the foundation deep in the bed of the creek and in the month of November there came one shower and I caught enough of water to saw eighty feet of lumber and then it began to snow and snowed one snow after another, till it was four feet on a level and drifted till it covered the stake and ridered fences and in many places was seven or eight feet deep. On my farm, too, it took two good yoke of oxen to haul one shock of fodder and continued so till in February, 1831.

Before his death, Mr. Cantrall gathered some material for a family history, and I am told that he requested the book to be published after his death. I have been unable to find any of these papers.

Levi Cantrall was married twice. There were thirteen children in the first family and two in the last: Thomas, Ann, Nancy, Steven L., Celindra, Eleanor, Elizabeth, Levi L., Rachel, Charles S., Joshua L., Jessie, McDonald, Fannie L., Joseph S.

THOMAS CANTRALL

Was born October 11, 1810. Died June 22, 1856. Married Priscilla D. McLemore October 3, 1831. She was born September 14, 1814. They had nine children: Clarissa, Turner H., Young M., Levi, Nancy A., Thomas J., Fannie P., Mary E., James D.

CLARISSA CANTRALL was born January 20, 1833. Never married and makes her home at Athens, Ill.

TURNER H. CANTRALL was born May 9, 1834. Never married and died November 30, 1894, at his sister Nancy's, in Greensburg, Mo.

YOUNG M. CANTRALL was born April 30, 1836. Died July 1, 1863. Married Ellen Graham February 14, 1861. She was born September 6, 1838. Mr. Cantrall enlisted in 1862 in Co. C, 114th Illinois Infantry. Died in the army. Their only child, Thomas E., was born March 12, 1862. Married Grace

M. Whitney May 8, 1883. Their children are: Estella May, born February 11, 1885; Young A., born September 18, 1889; Ula J., born September 21, 1893, died November 2, 1893; Allen W., born October 7, 1894. Mr. Cantrall is a school teacher.

LEVI CANTRALL was born July 16, 1838. Died March 21, 1861. He was a cripple and died at his brother Turner's at Elkhart Ill.

NANCY A. CANTRALL was born March 25, 1840. Married Egbert Mallory August, 1858. Their children are: Thomas, Egbert, Ormand, Minnie R., Angie, Benjamin F. Thomas Mallory died when about 28 years old. Egbert O., married Minnie Frogg. Minnie R. married Albert Petit. They had one daughter. Angie married Mr. Frogg. All live near Greensburg, Mo.

THOMAS J. CANTRALL was born December 21, 1842. He served three years in the 10th Illinois Cavalry, re-enlisted and served one year and four months more, was honorably discharged. Married Bell Dye. They have three children and live in Oklahoma.

FANNIE P. CANTRALL was born March 2, 1844. Died May 6, 1888. Married James D. Mallory April 25, 1861. Their children are: Henry E., and Edwin Archer. Henry E. Mallory is married, has two children and lives at Jerseyville, Ill. Mr. Mallory is a railroad mail agent.

Edwin A. Mallory is in the government employ in Chicago, Ill.

MARY E. CANTRALL was born December 8, 1844. For 25 years she taught school in Sangamon and Menard counties. Never married and lives in Jacksonville, Ill.

JAMES D. CANTRALL was born January 11, 1847. Died in infancy.

Mrs. Priscilla Cantrall died and Thomas married Elizabeth Estiel June 12, 1848. She was born January 28, 1820. They had four children: Martha E., Robert H., William Mack, Charles.

MARTHA E. CANTRALL was born June 12, 1849. Married David Van Deventer October 1, 1869. They had one child, Emma, born October 21, 1871. Her mother died when she was 6 months old and she was raised by her Grandmother Cantrall.

ROBERT H. CANTRALL was born July 16, 1851. Married Louisa A. Goff August 14, 1873. She was born July 11, 1853. They have eight children: Effie Bell, born February 27, 1874; Thomas Arthur was born July 3, 1875. Married Sylvia Potter September 23, 1896. They had one child, Roy Irvin, born August 1, 1897. Lilly Jane, born February 17, 1877. Married Frank Brown August 5, 1896. Minnie Etta was born December 15, 1878; Robert Earnest was born July 19, 1880, died April 15, 1881. Stella May was born January 18, 1882; Luther Franklin was born December 23, 1883; Goff Estiel, born November 15, 1894. Mr. Cantrall lives on a farm just outside of the eastern limits of Athens, Ill.

WILLIAM M. CANTRALL was born April 16, 1853. Married Mary Letitia McLelland March 22, 1882. She was born October 22, 1864. Their children are: Bessie Helen, born March 4, 1883; Earl Esta, born May 21, 1885; Raymond Leslie, born January 16, 1887; Rena May, born April 12, 1888. Died September 1, 1892. Archie Lee, born May 1, 1890. Percy Wilson was born April 18, 1892. Ruth Hester was born December 3, 1893. Fred McDonald was born August 21, 1895. Mr. Cantrall is a farmer and dairyman and lives just outside the southern limits of Springfield, Ill.

CHARLES H. CANTRALL was born December 29, 1855. He with his mother and niece, Emma Van Deventer, live on a farm near Fancy Prairie, Ill.

Thomas Cantrall lost his life by a runaway team dragging a saw-log over him.

ANN CANTRALL

Was born July 27, 1812. Married Edward Ridgway. They had three children, Nancy, Eliza, and a son died in infancy. Nancy Ridgway married James Milan. They live

50

near Elkhart, Illinois.   Mr. Ridgway died and his widow married Ferdinand Meeker.   They had one daughter, Dulcina. She married H. Jeremiah Lashbaugh.

NANCY CANTRALL

Was born September 13, 1813.   Died November 27, 1850. Married Turner Holland, February, 1832.   He was born July 17, 1806.   Died, March 6, 1866.   Their children, Amanda, Thomas, Fannie, Milam, Marian, William H., Benjamin F., Lucinda, Priscilla, Levi.

AMANDA HOLLAND was born May 30, 1833.   Married Elias B. Fench.   Her only child died in infancy, and she died April 3, 1854.

THOMAS HOLLAND died in infancy.

FANNY HOLLAND was born December 5, 1835.   Married Thomas R. Claypool, October 8, 1854.   He was born February 19, 1826.   Their children, Ida M., Clara B., Charles H., Levi B., Chloe L., Fredie D.

Ida M. Claypool was born April 2, 1857.   Married C. C. Van Meter, October 13, 1874.   They have two children, Hattie Bell, born June 14, 1876; Abram D., born May 7, 1879.   Mr. VanMeter lives on a farm 4 miles east of Cantrall, Ill.

Clara B. Claypool was born May 14, 1859.   Married John Dolvin December 25, 1888.   They have one child, Joy V., born May 17, 1894.

Charles H. Claypool was born June 18, 1863.   Died January 28, 1864.   Levi B. Claypool was born June 9, 1865.   Married Lena England September 8, 1887.   Their children, Harry E. was born January 29, 1889.   Died, December 8, 1891. Joseph F. was born June, 1891.   Robert, born July, 1892. Ellis was born February 7, 1894.   Luvena born December 7, 1895.

Chloe L. Claypool was born July 14, 1867, and Fredie D. Claypool was born December 21, 1871.   Live with their parents.   Their home is adjoining Cantrall on the north very near where Levi Cantrall settled.

MILAM HOLLAND was born July 19, 1837. Married Mary A. England, and died about one month after marriage. His widow married Wellington Mott.

FRANCIS MARIAN HOLLAND born March 2, 1839. Died when 18 years old.

WILLIAM H. HOLLAND was born October 28, 1840. Married Ruth A. Canterberry, February 12, 1867. They had several children, but all died in infancy, except Albert and Charley. Charley was killed by a horse when about ten years old. Albert Holland is married and lives in the mountains of Western Wyoming. The parents live at Buffalo, Wyoming.

BENJAMIN F. HOLLAND was born July 8, 1842. Married Maggie R. Hunt December 28, 1865. She was born September 30, 1843. Their children are: Thomas C., born December 29, 1869. Married Clara Ishmael October 21, 1893. Mr. Holland is a telegraph operator and lives at Wichita, Kansas. Eddie G., born October 15, 1873, is ticket agent at Oakford, Ill. Thomas Holland was born July 19, 1877. Lives with his parents at Cantrall, Ill.

LUCINDA HOLLAND was born February 17, 1844. Married James I. Woods, March 1, 1866. They had one child, James I., Jr. Mr. Woods died July 2, 1870. His widow married Charles Calhoon. They have one child, Agnes, and live at Sheridan, Wyo.

PRISCILLA HOLLAND was born March 17, 1846. Married William S. Hurt, February 1, 1866. He was born January 4, 1846. Their children are: Harry T., born July 28, 1867. He is married and has one child and lives in Genevia, Ind. James F., born September, 1869, is a railroad man. Fred Grant was born May, 1872, and lives at Fort Worth, Texas. Is a railroad man at Auburn Park, Chicago. Mr. Hurt lives at Kingfisher, Oklahoma Territory.

LEVI HOLLAND was born May, 1848. Died when about 2 years old.

STEPHEN L. CANTRALL

Was born April 4, 1815. Died July, 1875. Married Mary Ridgway, 1833. Their children are: Fannie, Almira, Jane, George W.

FANNIE CANTRALL was born January 26, 1835. Married George R. Provin December 13, 1850. Their children are: Sarah M., Laura A., Joel Wesley, Viena Ellen, George W., Stephen Clark, Ulysses Grant, Savilla Prose, John R.

Sarah M. Provin was born October 16, 1851. Married John P. North December 30, 1865. Their children are: Jessie G., born October 4, 1867; William E., born July 15, 1870; Fannie J., born April 6, 1873; Viola E., born December 27, 1878; Harry S., born October 29, 1882; Bertie C., born June 11, 1888. Mr. North lives at Lane Station, Ill.

Laura A. Provin was born November 26, 1853. Married Watson Newberry September 8, 1874. Their children are: L. A., born January 4, 1876; Minnie J., born December 17, 1878; Lulu A., born January 26, 1880. Mr. Newberry died December 13, 1894, and his widow lives at Clinton, Ill.

Joel W. Provin, born June 12, 1866. Married Jane S. Webb March 24, 1878. Their children are: Perry, born 1878; Laura, born 1881; Ira, born 1889; Homer, born 1894. Mr. Provin lives near Clinton, Ill.

V. Ellen Provin, born March 7, 1859. Married Daniel Lukenbill November, 1881. Their children are: Ora F., born August 30, 1876; Liddie, born October 8, 1883; Sydney, born February 7, 1886; Rosa Nell, born January 16, 1889; Pearl, born September 13, 1894; Ruby, born November 25, 1896. They live at Weldon, Ill.

George W. Provin was born February 3, 1862. Married Katie E. Smith February 17, 1897. They have one child, Smith Sydney, born December 31, 1897. They live at Malcom, Ia.

Stephen C. Provin, born March 3, 1866. Married Jacobina N. Knutson August 17, 1895. They have one child, Syble May. Their home is at Howe, Ia.

Ulysses G. Provin was born September 29, 1868. Married Emma West February 28, 1894. Their children are: Clarence R., Clyde E., Roy O. Live at Malcom, Ia.

Savilla P. Provin was born June 13, 1872. Died February 29, 1888.

John R. Provin, born January 20, 1878. Died in infancy.

ALMIRA J. CANTRALL was born February 22, 1837. Died 1857. Married Samuel Mellinger. They had one child, Samuel L., born January 30, 1856. He married Mary J. Dorshman March 1, 1877. She was born November 9, 1860. Their children are: Samuel L., born July 19, 1878; Minerva A., born March 9, 1880; Mahala D., born November 5, 1882. Mrs. Mellinger died July 12, 1886. Mr. Mellinger married Margaret Miller. Five children were born to them: Floyd, Willie, Oliver, Lucy, Rose. Mr. Mellinger died September 28, 1895. His widow lives near DeWitt, Ill.

Samuel Mellinger married Maranda Snelson, whose maiden name was Cantrall. See her name.

GEORGE W. CANTRALL was born September 9, 1839. Died June 29, 1863. He enlisted in 1862 in Co. I, 114th Illinois Infantry, and died at 13 A. C. hospital, at Chickasaw Bluffs, Miss.

CELINDRA CANTRALL

Was born November 14, 1816. Died young.

ELEANOR CANTRALL

Was born October 17, 1818. Married John Jordan. She died in Kansas in 1893 and he died about six months after. Could not learn any more.

ELIZABETH E. CANTRALL

Was born May 26, 1820. Married James Driskell. He was born January 20, 1814. Their children are: Abram V., Levi C., David S., Sarah C., Harriet Jane, Elizabeth. Mr. Driskell died November 10, 1862. His wife died May 25, 1850.

ABRAM V. DRISKELL married Maggie Williams. They had one son, George W., born March, 1877. His home was Los Angeles, Cal. He left for Klondyke February, 1898.

LEVI C. DRISKELL was born July 30, 1841. Never married and lives with his sister, Harriet Fulkerson.

DAVID S. DRISKELL was born in 1843. He enlisted in 1862, came home and died, from diseases contracted in the army, at the home of McDonald Cantrall.

SARAH C. DRISKELL was born January 17, 1846. Married Harrison Hurt. Their children are: Eleanor P., born October 14, 1865; Hattie died in infancy; Annie, born July 7, 1868.

Eleanor P. Hurt married Thomas Hines. They have four children: Harry, Oscar, Helen, Thurman. They live at David City, Neb.

Anna Hurt married George Hutchison. They have one child, David Glenn, and live at Wymore, Neb.

Harrison Hurt died August 16, 1868. His widow married John Kennedy. Their children are: Laura Bell is married and lives at Payson, Ill.; David is single and is a book-keeper at Freeport, Ill; Homer is in the army; Frank, Grace, Ralph, Iles, Thomas, Flavia Scott. Their home is at Payson, Ill.

HARRIET JANE DRISKELL, born November 3, 1848. Married Abram Fulkinson August 7, 1867. He was born August 27, 1839. His father lives in Williamsville, Ill., and will be 99 years old September 12, 1898. Their children are: Clara Frances was born July 22, 1868. Married Charles D. Becker May 22, 1892. They have two children: Abram E., born June 28, 1893; Helen L., born February 28, 1895.

James William was born October 27, 1871. Married Angeline Constant February 16, 1897. They have one child, born July 5, 1898.

Sarah E., born October 7, 1873. Died in infancy. Frank D., born September 7, 1876. Died March 5, 1879.

ELIZABETH DRISKELL was born April 17, 1859. Married John W. Graham November 1, 1866. He was born February 22, 1845. Their children are: Albert Y., born October 29, 1867. Lives in Jacksonville, Ill. Mary E., born November 27, 1869. Lives in Williamsville, Ill. Hattie Agnes, born June 24, 1871. Married Clayton R. Hartley March 31, 1896.

He was born April 7, 1863. They have one child, John Alexander, born January 18, 1897. Mr. Hartley is in the livery business in Williamsville, Ill.

Mrs. Elizabeth Graham married John McClelland September 1, 1879. He was born December 1, 1825. Their children are: Charles Benjamin, born February 27, 1881; Daisy Bell, born October 14, 1882, died while young.

LEVI L. CANTRALL

Was born March 17, 1822. Died March 15, 1863. Married Elizabeth C. King. She was born July 11, 1828. Died May 7, 1896. Their children are: Jasper H., William M., John T., Mary E., Alfred Newton

JASPER H. CANTRALL, born March 23, 1847. Married Sarah E. Waggoner July 2, 1868. She was born December 25, 1849. Their children are: William H., Bertram F., Joseph W., Alfred L., Ethel B.

William H. Cantrall was born August 24, 1869. Married Adaline Cate 1890. Their children are: Lulu Fay, born January 25, 1893. Louis, born January 11, 1895. They live in Trenton, Mo.

Bertam F. Cantrall was born November 7, 1872. Married Addie Herrin March 16, 1892. Their children are: Frank, born January 28, 1893; Lucile, born July 25, 1896. They live in Athens, Ill.

Joseph W. Cantrall, born December 31, 1874. Lives in Meadowville, Mont.

Alfred L. Cantrall, born September 14, 1877; Ethel B. Cantrall, born September 27, 1881. Live with their parents in Athens, Ill.

WILLIAM M. CANTRALL was born March 1, 1849. Died January 17, 1895. Married Minnie Wells. She died July 6, 1889. Their children are: Alvin N., Virgie, Pearl, Lillie, Grace, Grover, Leona, George, and one died in infancy. There homes is near Otterbein, Ind.

John T. Cantrall was born February 20, 1851. Died May 27, 1852.

Mary E. Cantrall was born February 16, 1863. Married Benjamin F. Warren, September 2, 1874. Their children are: Harry N., Fanny. Cora, Jessie, Benjamin, Everest, Rosa, Clarence, Verna. They live at Illiopolis, Ill.

Alfred N. Cantrall was born March 18, 1855. Married Alice Mathews February 24, 1881. She was born December 26, 1859. Their children are: Lloyd L., born December 16, 1881. Margie May, born September 12, 1884. Weller J., born August 30, 1886. Ross B., born June 20, 1888. Jennie Taylor born August 5, 1891. Thomas Lee, born December 27, 1893. Myron Mathew, born April 11, 1898. They live in Athens, Ill.

RACHEL CANTRALL

Was born February 8, 1824. Married John Overstreet, May 11, 1839. They have four living children: Louisa J., James W., Elizabeth A., John T.

Louisa J. Overstreet was born May 11, 1841. Married Henry F. Shepherd. Both died leaving one child, Louisa. She married Jeff Bennett and died leaving one daughter.

James W. Overstreet was born February 5, 1844. Married Mrs. Martha E. Dunlap. Their children are: Jennie, Mary, Nellie.

Elizabeth A. Overstreet was born June 13, 1848. Married by Sebastian E. Shepherd, December 5, 1866. Their children, Louisa S., Emma L., Lavina G. Mr. Shepherd enlisted in 1862 in Co. K, 115th Illinois Infantry. Served three full years and was honorably discharged. Lives at Athens, Ill.

John T. Overstreet was born November 15, 1851. Married Maggie Brenan December 24, 1872. Both are dead and their two daughters are living at Lincoln, Ill.

CHARLES S. CANTRALL

Was born January 6, 1826. Died December 18, 1875. Married Emily M. Vandegrift, January 7, 1845. They had two children, Mary E., McDonald.

Mary E. Cantrall was born June 13, 1848. Married Stephen O. Price January 25, 1866. He was born January 24, 1847. They have two children, Emily, Ellen, William, Oscar. Mr. Price lives on a farm four miles east of Lincoln, Ill.

Emily E. Price married A. F. Reed, March 14, 1889. Their children, Roy William, born March 7, 1890; Raymond Price, Ralph, Mabel. Their home is at Bement, Ill.

William O. Price was born May 29, 1870. Married Lida Section November 24, 1892. She was born June 30, 1871. They have one child, May Irene. Born February 2, 1895. Mr. Price is in the livery business at Lincoln, Ill.

McDonald Cantrall was born August 20, 1851. Married Margaret M. Peden, August 4, 1870. She was born January 14, 1854. Their children are: Maude A., born September 16, 1871. Married G. M. Mathews, January 21, 1894. Henry A., born February 9, 1874. He is in the army. Bruce T., born May 9, 1878. Josiah P., born April 5, 1881. Betrix N., born August 10, 1883. Tracy E., born August 1, 1885. She was killed by a wagon running over her September 7, 1895. Mr. Cantrall is postmaster at Illiopolis, Ill.

Mrs. Emily M. Cantrall died January 29, 1852, and Charles S. married for his second wife Lucy A. Swearengen June 29, 1852. They had one child, Minerva A., born March 25, 1853. Died August 20, 1853. Her mother died April 14, 1853.

Charles S. Cantrall married for his third wife Harriet A. Graham April 26, 1855. She was born February 17, 1836. Their children are: Charles H., Thomas D., Allie, John W., Levi G., William H., Fannie A., Homer E., Ida May, Ira.

Charles H. Cantrall, born March 12, 1856. Married Viola Batterton April 28, 1898. She was born November 30, 1871. Mr. Cantrall is in the grocery business in Athens, Ill.

Thomas D. Cantrall, born December 15, 1858. Married Mary F. Enlow January 30, 1884. She was born November 1, 1863. Their children are: Thomas Leroy, born April 5, 1885; Charles Raymond, born August 13, 1887, died October 11, 1887; Anna Lynn, born October 2, 1890. Mr. Cantrall is partner with his brother in the grocery business at Athens, Ill.

Allie Cantrall, born January 14, 1861. Lives with her mother.

John W. Cantrall, born April 8, 1863. Married Alma V. Prophater April 29, 1896. Mr. Cantrall is a physician at Illiopolis, Ill.

Levi G. Cantrall, born September 8, 1865. Married Ella Norred March 6, 1888. Their children are: Guy, born December 19, 1889; Wilbur, born April 15, 1891; Mira, born August 19, 1894. Their home is in Illiopolis, Ill.

William H. Cantrall, born November 28, 1867. Married Nannie Muir March 1, 1895. They live on a farm near Illiopolis, Ill.

Fannie A. Cantrall, born February 3, 1870. Married William J. Tackett March 24, 1892. Their children are: Charles Leland, born December 13, 1892; Tracey James, born December 18, 1894. Their home is near Willeys Station.

Homer E. Cantrall, born July 6, 1872. Married Bernice Johnson April 26, 1897. They have one child, Horace. Their home is at Taylorville, Ill.

Ida M. Cantrall, born March 29, 1874. Died November 25, 1875.

Ira Cantrall, born July 1, 1877. Lives on the farm with his mother and sister Allie.

JOSHUA L. CANTRALL

Was born July 28, 1828. Died March 17, 1882. Married Rebecca Hedrick October 16, 1847. She was born October 8, 1828. Their children are: Lafayette, Fannie C., Carlyle, Charles, Barton R., Parthena, Julia, McDonald C., Laura E., Clara P., Levi, Benjamin F., Jennie.

Lafayette Cantrall, born January 16, 1849. Married Gussie Chambers July 23, 1874. She was born April 11, 1856. They live near Illiopolis, Ill.

Fannie C. Cantrall, born September 9, 1850. Married Benjamin F. Capps August 12, 1869. October 8, 1869 she was killed by a horse. While talking with friends the horse became frightened and the loop of the halter strap was tightly drawn around her wrist and she was dragged until dead.

CARLYLE CANTRALL, born May 26, 1852. Married Alice Ina King October 12, 1876. She was born December 3, 1853. They have one child, Ruth Macie, born October 12, 1877. In 1896, she graduated from the college of music, Jacksonville, Ill.

CHARLES CANTRALL, born December 23, 1853. Died in infancy.

BARTON R. CANTRALL, born April 26, 1856; is single and makes his home with his mother.

PARTHENA CANTRALL, born May 30, 1858; died in infancy.

JULIA CANTRALL, born April 11, 1860; was married to Hardy Council, December 5, 1883. Their children are: J. Russel, born April 2, 1885; Hardy E., born May 4, 1890; La-Fayette M., born July 27, 1892; Clara Florence, born December 15, 1893.

McDONALD C. CANTRALL, born January 1, 1862; is single and lives with his mother.

LAURA E. CANTRALL, born June 3, 1864. Married Josiah Todd, March 22, 1883. They have one child, Fred, born May 24, 1884. Mr. Todd died March 10, 1884, and she married Archie Dickerson, January 2, 1886. They have one child, Erastus, born, January 20, 1898.

CLARA P. CANTRALL, born September 8, 1866. Married Charles J. Campbell December 5, 1888. Their children are: Owen Henry, born September 12, 1889. Helen, born September 16, 1895. Mr. Campbell was born March 29, 1859.

LEVI CANTRALL, born April 20, 1868. Married Eva Colvin, July 20, 1892. She was born March 26, 1872. Their child, Lelah, was born July 16, 1893. Died July 25, 1894.

BENJAMIN F. CANTRALL, born August 25, 1870. Married Fanny Burch Adams, January 8, 1895. She was born January 27, 1873. They have one child, Grace, born April 2, 1897.

JENNIE CANTRALL, born June 13, 1872; died in infancy.

Joshua's widow lives in Illiopolis. Ill., and all her children live near her except Julia, who lives near Elkhart, Ill.

JESSE CANTRALL

Was born April 7, 1830. Married Eliza J. Humes. Their children, Martha, Rachel, Jefferson, Ann, Fannie E., Mary Jane, Johnnie, Jessie, Ella, Ida, Joshua, Cora.

MARTHA CANTRALL, married Omer Tibbets. She died, leaving two children, Albert and Nettie. They live at Ochletree, Kan.

RACHEL CANTRALL married William Tibbets. They have three children: Jessie May, Adolph, Charlie. Their home is Ochletree, Kan.

JEFFERSON CANTRALL married Julia Mead. Their children, William, Walter, Jessie, Elmer. They live at Ochletree, Kan.

ANN CANTRALL married Wallace Wilson. Their children, Wilmot, Cora.

FANNIE E. CANTRALL married John Caswell. Their children, Charlie, Harry, Lee.

MARY JANE CANTRALL married William Burgess. They have four children and live in Olathe, Kan.

JOHNNIE CANTRALL died when 22 years old.

ELLA CANTRALL married George Green. They have two children and live at Monroe City, Mo.

JESSIE CANTRALL married Laura Studerville. They live in Oklahoma.

IDA CANTRALL married Jasper Burgess. They have two children and live in Olathe, Kan.

JOSHUA and CORA CANTRALL are at home at Black Bob, Kan.

McDONALD CANTRALL

Was born April 5, 1833. Died September 15, 1872. Married Narcissa Hedrick March 29, 1854. They had one child, CHARLES, born February 14, 1855. Married Florence Council May 16, 1888. She was born June 4, 1867. Their children are: John Harry, born May 4, 1889, and McDonald, born February

2, 1897. Mr. Cantrall lives on a farm four and one-half miles northeast of Cantrall, Ill.

Mrs. Fannie Cantrall died September 10, 1835, and Levi Cantrall married Mrs. Ann Barnett, whose maiden name was Patterson, May 27, 1836. She was born September 29, 1803. Their children are: Fannie L., and Joseph S.

FANNIE L. CANTRALL

Was born October 9, 1838. Married Henry C. Graham January 6, 1857. He was born May 6, 1833. Their children are: Mary A., William H., Araminta, Joseph S. and Carrie.

MARY A. GRAHAM, born June 23, 1858. Married William E. Johnson September 14, 1882. Their children are: Mildred, born August 10, 1883; Addie, born June 7, 1885; Minnie, born August 26, 1887. Mr. Johnson lives on a farm near Athens, Ill.

WILLIAM H. GRAHAM, born August 11, 1862. Married Anna L. Clark January 10, 1884. Their children are: Edith L., born November 2, 1884; Owen C., born June 12, 1888. Mrs. Anna E. Graham died January 14, 1889, and Mr. Graham married Phoebe Hardman May 9, 1895. Their children are: W. Harrold, born May 23, 1896, and Paul H., born May 9, 1898. Mr. Graham is a farmer and stock raiser and lives near Athens, Ill.

ARAMINTA GRAHAM, born October 13, 1868. Married Harry Fulton May 3, 1893. He was born December 2, 1867. They have one child, Fannie L., born August 13, 1895. Mr. Fulton is a farmer and lives near Athens, Ill.

JOSEPH S. GRAHAM, born March 26, 1871. Married Lillian N. Primm January 16, 1895. They have one child, Henry P., born November 25, 1895. Mr. Graham is a farmer and lives near Athens, Ill.

CARRIE GRAHAM, born August 5, 1878. Married Webster H. VanMeter, July 13, 1898. Mr. Henry Graham lives five miles northeast of Athens, Ill.

JOSEPH S. CANTRALL, born October 16, 1841. Married Margaret A. Canterberry, January 14, 1869. She was born

January 10, 1849. Their children, Daisy L., Dora, Hattie May, Evans Earl.

Daisy L. (Dora) Cantrall, born February 15, 1870. Is a teacher of music.

Hattie May Cantrall, born March 5, 1875. Is supervisor of art instruction in the Springfield public schools, Springfield, Ill.

Evans E. Cantrall, born November 15, 1884. Joseph S. Cantrall lives at 526 South Walnut street, Springfield, Ill.

Levi Cantrall, died February 22, 1860, on the farm where he settled in 1819. The town of Cantrall, Ill., was laid out on the land he entered soon after he came, and was named in honor of his memory. His widow made her home with her son, Joseph, for 22 years. And died there, September 26, 1889.

WYATT CANTRALL.

The eighth son of Joshua Cantrall, was born December 20, 1790. Died October 25, 1877. Married Sally England. She was born December 20, 1794, died August 4, 1840. Their children are: Eliza, Samuel Denny, David P., Zebulon E., Wyatt E., Stephen England, William F., Polly Ann, John H.

ELIZA CANTRALL

Was born September 8, 1813. Married John McElmore. He died in 1871. His widow and two children live at Sterling, Ill. The children are: Clarence and Lucinda.

Lucinda McElmore married Almanza Merrill. They live in Reno, Marshall county, Nev.

SAMUEL D. CANTRALL

Was born February 9, 1816. Died May 1, 1884. Married Sarah S. Alexander March 6, 1837. She was born

November 7, 1820. Their children are: Albert A., Wiott E., Mary H., John S., Lucinda S., Henry, Eliza, Margaret A., and a daughter died in infancy.

ALBERT A. CANTRALL, born November 15, 1839. Served three years and died on the way home. Was in Andersonville prison. Died March 5, 1865. Married Martha Hurt March 6, 1862. There were no children and his widow lives in Athens, Ill.

WIOTT E. CANTRALL, born November 5, 1841. Died March 31, 1898. Married Grizilla Holland November 17, 1869. She was born April 9, 1848. Their children are: Anna Bell, born September 30, 1870; Ina May, born April 14, 1874; Hattie S., born November 26, 1883.

Annie B. Cantrall married Edgar McClelland January 24, 1889. He was born March 9, 1867. She died December 28, 1889, and he married her sister, Ina M., March 1, 1890. Their children are: Gracie May, born December 28, 1890; Hazel Marie, born June 22, 1894; Harry E., born March 19, 1897. Mr. McClelland lives with his wife's mother in Springfield, Ill.

MARY H. CANTRALL, born August 5, 1843. Died April 11, 1844.

JOHN S. CANTRALL, born February 1, 1845. Died October 1, 1845.

LUCINDA S. CANTRALL, born May 14, 1847. Married Frank Horn December 24, 1868. Their children are: Ira, Ida, Edward, Sarah, Alice, Ernest. They live at Hastings, Neb.

HENRY CANTRALL, born February 28, 1849. Married Emma E. Graham January 1, 1873. She was born September 6, 1853. Their children are: Alvin W., born December 1, 1873; Arthur W., born November 23, 1876; Verna E., born June 5, 1879; Samuel D., born January 1, 1882. Mr. Cantrall lives two miles east of Athens, Ill.

Alvin W. Cantrall married Allie Langford November 24, 1893. They have one child, Fay, and live in Springfield, Ill.

ELIZA CANTRALL, born April 18, 1852. Married Henry Lake July 7, 1874. Their children are: Maggie May, born May 27, 1875; Harvey H., born May 19, 1881, died January 1, 1892, and Elmer S., born December 8, 1882. Mr. Lake lives in Cantrall, Ill. His daughter, Maggie M., married James Vasconcelles March 15, 1898.- They live seven miles northeast of Lincoln, Ill.

MARGARET A. CANTRALL, born August 18, 1855. Married Isaac Bates December 10, 1873. Their children, Phronia, Ethel, Olive, Walter, and one died in infancy. Their home is Nortonville, Kan.

DAVID P. CANTRALL

Was born May 7, 1818. Died January 21, 1892. He was married twice. His first wife was Eleanor A. McLemore. Married March 13, 1841. She was born March 20, 1820; died January 15, 1861. Their children, Young M., Sarah E., Erastus D., Catherine.

YOUNG M. CANTRALL was born June 30, 1842. Married Emiline Buswel, February 5, 1865. She was born August 12, 1843. Died September 1, 1875. They had one child, George, born July 18, 1875. Mr. Cantrall married for his second wife Emma Hubbard, March 6, 1877. She was born May 6, 1856. Their children, Frank, born February 14, 1880; died October 22, 1887, and Gertrude, born July 26, 1891. Young M. Cantrall lives in Milledgeville, Ill.

SARAH E. CANTRALL, died August 20, 1845, while young.

ERASTUS D. CANTRALL died June 22, 1867, when 19 years old.

CATHERINE E. CANTRALL was born March 28, 1853. Married G. H. Riddle March 18, 1874. They have no children, and live near Rushville, Neb.

David P. Cantrall married for his second wife, Ursula Bull, June 5, 1861. She died August 25, 1894. Their children Eddie C., Wiott B., and Nettie C.

EDDIE C. CANTRALL was born February 16, 1863. Married Alexander C. Kirkpatrick February 9, 1887. A child was born May 24, 1897, and died in infancy. They live four miles southwest of Lisbon, Iowa.

WIOTT B. CANTRALL was born June 18, 1864. Married Maggie C. Snyder February 4, 1886. They had one son, Arthur Fay, born November 9, 1890; died November 20, 1890. They live on a farm near Sanborn, Iowa.

NETTIE C. CANTRALL was born November 12, 1865. Married Irvin H. Whitman, November 28, 1889. Their children, Clara Bell, born November 24, 1890; Frank, born December 3, 1892; Laura Eddie, born October 16, 1894, and Lue, born June 8, 1896. They live on a farm two miles south of Lisbon, Iowa.

ZEBULON E. CANTRALL

Was born August 11, 1823; died April, 1841.

WIOTT E. CANTRALL

Was born March 22, 1825; died August 1, 1840.

STEPHEN E. CANTRALL

Was born April 20, 1827. Married Caroline Blue. Their children WIOTT, ROBERT, JOHN, SCOTT, MARTHA, LILY. Stephen is dead. His widow lives in Hastings, Neb. Most of the children live near there.

WILLIAM F. CANTRALL

Was born July 28, 1829. Married Lucy Kingsberry. She died, and he married Calista Neil. They live in Iowa.

POLLY ANN CANTRALL,

Was born September 17, 1832. Married Devin Grimes. Their children are: LILLIAN and CHARLES. Her husband was wounded by the Indians and died soon after. Mrs. Grimes married Thomas Heathcoat. They have one son, WILLIAM, and live at Sterling, Ill.

JOHN H. CANTRALL

Was born October 1, 1834. Could not get further record.

Mrs. Sally Cantrall died August 1, 1840, and Wyatt married Mrs. Polly Kingsberry. They had one child, Joshua P. He married Grace Winters. They had one child. This is all the record I could find.

Samuel Cantrall, the ninth and youngest son of Joshua Cantrall, was born April 20, 1793. Died July 24, 1795.

———————

The following families, of which I only have very brief records, I have reasons to believe are related to the foregoing families, but of this I have no direct proof. It is said that Levi Cantrell and William Centrill visited each other and were satisfied they were cousins, but I can not tell how. Pinkney Cantrell, in his letter, says he is sure that we are related, but are unable to say just how. I trust any one who can give my any record or information concerning these families will please write me at Irvington, Ind., all they know, or can find out about the tribe, as it is my purpose to make a more complete record. I met T. E. Cantrell and family, of San Francisco, California, but could trace no relationship. I have heard that there are many Cantralls in Kentucky, but I have not come in touch with them. By your help, I may be able, at no distant day, to make a more perfect record of so large a family.

THOMAS CANTRILL.

— ..

Was born April 4, 1775. Married Elizabeth Murray. She was born September 19, 1774. Died October 1, 1836. He died October 3, 1836. They moved from Kentucky in 1838 to Sangamon county, Ill., four and one-half miles east of Springfield. Their children: Mary, William, Zebulon, Susan, Ann, Joel.

MARY CANTRALL was born December 23, 1797. She died February 7, 1874. Married Thomas Perry. He died February 11, 1869, in his 79th year. They married in Kentucky and came to Illinois before her parents. Their children, RACHEL PERRY, died December 28, 1868, in her 50th year; never married.

MARY J. PERRY married James Crowley. She was born May 26, 1838. Died January 13, 1872.

LOUISA PERRY, born Feburay 5, 1828. Died September 14, 1836.

JOHN H. PERRY, born June 1, 1831. Died October 14, 1825.

L. ANN PERRY, married Andrew Barnhill. Died, March 27, 1862, in her 39th year. They had one child, Mary J., born September 25, 1845; died May 20, 1871.

WILLIAM CANTRILL

Born January 17, 1800, in Green county, Kentucky. Died November 26, 1881. Moved to Springfield, Ill., in March, 1825. Married Elizabeth Hall, February 14, 1828. She was born December 18, 1809; died August 4, 1868. Moved to Decatur, Ill., in 1833. Their children, Thomas Hall, Jane Ellen, Mary Elizabeth, Susan, Lavinia, Anna.

THOMAS H. CANTRILL, born November 1, 1829, in Sangamon County. Was raised in Decatur; attended the Illinois College at Jacksonville, Ill., and went to California in 1852. Married in Walla Walla, Washington, was accidentally drowned in the Columbia river, British Columbia, 1864. His wife died about the same time. They left three children. All married and have families, and live somewhere in the northwest.

JANE E. CANTRILL, born October 27, 1832. Married Dr. A. L. Keller, April 14, 1852. She died October, 1892, in Sullivan, Ill. They had eight children, three of whom died in infancy. Addie, the oldest daughter, married Dr. J. M. Goodwin, moved to Palmona, Cal., where she died in 1894. Charles H., the oldest son, is a painter by trade, and lives in Sullivan, Ill. Edgar Harland Keller, born June 18, 1863. Married Lida Stewart, April 14, 1866. Their children, Stewart, born in 1889; Mary Jane, born in 1892; Namoah, born in 1896. Mr. Keller is a minister of the Gospel, and lives at Waxahachie, Tex.

Elizabeth M. Keller married a Mr. Thompson and lives in California.

Notie Pearl Keller, born July 14, 1875. Married R. C. Flemming April 14, 1896. He was born October 18, 1872. Mr. Fleming is assistant ticket agent at Springfield, Ill., for the Wabash Railroad.

MARY E. CANTRILL, born September 27, 1835. Died October 26, 1883. Married William Dillon. He died in June, 1889, at Quincy, Ill. They were married April 14, 1854. Their children, William Thomas, Louis Edward, Fannie, Frank, Ella May, George Jeffreys, Mary E., Robert Lee, Anna S., Parthenia Jane, Grace.

W. T. Dillon, born January 9, 1855. Married Jennie Gillespie, January 9, 1877. Their children, Don C., Nellie May, Earnest. Mr. Dillon lives at Chicago, Ill.

Louis E. Dillon, born October 5, 1857. Married Henrietta Edmonds. Their children, Roy, who lives at Quincy, Ill., and is deputy sheriff of Adams county. George died in infancy.

Fannie Dillon, who died in infancy.

Frank Dillon, born October 11, 1860. Lives in Chicago, Ill.

Ella M. Dillon died in infancy.

George J. Dillon, born July 26, 1863. Married Marion Irvington. They had one child, Duncan William. He lives at Cook, Neb.

Mary E. Dillon, born November 30, 1867. Married George M. Reed, April 14, 1887. Their children, Kenneth Samuel and Miriam. Their home is 1111 South 3d Ave., Omaha, Neb.

Robert L. Dillon, born November 14, 1870. Is unmarried and lives at San Francisco, Cal.

Anna S. Dillon, born November 14, 1871. Married Charles C. Williams August 20, 1891. They have one child, Leland Thomas. Their home is Hoopston, Ill.

Parthenia J. Dillon, born March 14, 1873. Died July 16, 1890.

Grace C. Dillon, born May 16, 1876. Lives at Hoopeston, Ill.

Susan L. Cantrill, born July 3, 1844. Married Harland P. Christie, at Decatur, Ill. Their children: Louie Cantrill and Harland William. Their home is 231 Madison street, Brooklyn Borough, New York City.

SUSAN CANTRILL

Married Robert Bird. They had two children and the parents died.

ANN CANTRILL

Married William Black. Their children, William C., born February 29, 1845. Died August 30, 1845. The other children are: Joel, Palace, Sarah.

ZEBULON CANTRILL,

Born April 8, 1807. Married Elizabeth Enyart. They had four children. He died January 8, 1840.

JOEL CANTRILL

Was born January 8, 1811. Died September 4, 1866. Married Zerelda E. Branch, May 16, 1839. She was born November 19, 1831. Their children: Lewis M., Edward T., William D., James N., Laura Jane, Henrietta and Henry A., twins, Emily B, Charles, Benjamin H.

LEWIS M. CANTRILL, born April 9, 1840. Married Almira Lee. They have no children and live at North Bangor, N. Y.

EDWARD T. CANTRILL, born December 20, 1842. Enlisted in the army, took sick at Vicksburg, and died a few days after the surrender. Died July 11, 1863.

WILLIAM D. CANTRILL, born November 22, 1845. Married Elizabeth S. Derry October 7, 1875. She was born December 9, 1852. They had one child, born May 29, 1887. Died in infancy. Their home is four and one-half miles east of Springfield, Ill.

JAMES N. CANTRILL, born March 17, 1848. Married Anna S. Waters, March 19, 1874. She was born December 19, 1850. Their children, Charles Edward, born December 4, 1874, Nellie Ulelah, born February 23, 1877, Louemna, born February 20, 1879; Frank S., born March 22, 1882, died in infancy, Lizzie Maud, born November 15, 1888.

Charles E. Cantrill is cashier of the Citizens' State Bank, Edinburg, Ill.

Nellie U. Cantrill is teacher in the public schools in Edinburg, Ill. The family lives at Edinburg, Ill.

LAURA JANE CANTRILL died when 15 years old.

HENRIETTA CANTRILL, born January 9, 1853. Married W. H. Colby October 7, 1874. He was born September 14, 1879. Their children: Charles Percy, born November 5, 1875; Honoretta Bertha, born March 19, 1878; Laura Mabel, born September 6, 1884; George Bergen, born September 17, 1882; Catherine Uella, born October 17, 1888.

Charles P. Colby was a soldier in the late war with Spain.

W. H. Colby is an attorney in Springfield, Ill.

HENRY A. CANTRILL, born January 9, 1853. Married Eva Viola Harris, August 22, 1883, born October 21, 1857. Their children: Edward Thomas, born September 1, 1884; Parkeson Harris, born May 28, 1868; Allen Bradford, born September 30, 1888. Mr. Cantrill is a farmer and lives on the farm improved by his father, four and one-half miles southeast of Springfield, Ill.

EMILY B. CANTRILL, born September 7, 1855. Married Thomas Benton Hart, September 6, 1882. He was born April 17, 1858. They have no children. Mr. Hart is a fine stock raiser and lives at Edinburg, Ill.

CHARLES CANTRILL, born October 31, 1857; died October 31, 1858.

BENJAMIN H. CANTRILL, born September 24, 1859; died August 30, 1860.

The following is a record furnished me of a Cantrell family by Pinkney Cantrell, of Billings, Mo. His grandfather was Aaron Cantrell. He was a North Carolinian. Aaron had one brother, Sampson, and a sister, Katie.

Aaron Cantrell had five boys, William, John, Ephram, Moses, Smith.

Katie Cantrell married John Martin, long since died. Have no record of Sampson.

Ephram, father of Pinkney, had eight sons, Hiram, Lavin, Pinkney, Parris, Tahua, Milton, LaFayette, Howard Gerome, Elmore, Fulton.

Pinkney was born October 26, 1824. Has four sons, Ganswite, Thomas Pinkney, Benjamin Franklin, Edward Alphonso.

Alphonso Cantrell is a Christian preacher, and is located now at Vacaville, Cal. He was born May 30, 1872.

Pinkney Cantrell writes also that Tilman Cantrell was a Christian preacher, when he was but a boy, and that he was a distant relative of his father. He had two sons, William and David, both doctors.

Would be glad to receive any further record of this family that any one can furnish me.

A letter addressed to G. W. and John Cantrell brought the following: John Cantrell's father's name was Thomas. He had a brother George, but they are both dead. There were others also, but he did not mention their names. The following record was furnished by G. W. Cantrell, son of John, son of Thomas. Thomas Cantrell's children are: Thomas and Robert, of Monticello, N. Y.; John and William, of Monticello, N. Y.; Ann (now Brannom), of Warren, Pa.; Eliza (now Randel), of Monticello, N. Y.; Susie (now Bowers), of Toledo, Ohio.

John Cantrell's children are: George, William, Julia May, David W.

George W. Cantrell, born September 4, 1866. Married Clarissa E. Yoakam, February 8, 1891. Their children: Ada Bell, born January 23, 1892; Ruth May, born October 13, 1897. Their home is Brooklyn, Ohio. Mr. Cantrell is a civil engineer.

Julia May Cantrell, now Julia Porter, has one son, Walter; lives at Greenfield, Pa.

David W. Cantrell lives at Columbus Grove, Ohio.

BIRTHS

Name	*Place*	*Date*

MARRIAGES

Names	Place	Date

DEATHS

Name	Place	Date

.... THE ....

Northwestern Mutual
LIFE INSURANCE
COMPANY.

Purely Mutual and transacting business only in the
United States.

Statement Jan. 1 1898.

Assets,	$103,375,536
Liabilities, ·	80,885,093
Accumulations held to meet Tontine Policy contracts,	$16,310,434
General Surplus ·	6,180,009
Income,	$20,020,162
Insurance Written.	$61,187,593
Insurance Gained,	28,913,541
Policies in Force. ·	178,462
Insurance in Force,	$413,081,370

The Northwestern Mutual Life of Milwaukee,

IS recognized as being the BEST DIVIDEND PAYING COM-
PANY IN THE UNITED STATES. Under its NEW POLICY,
containing guaranteed Loan, Cash Value and extended insurance privileges, the dividends may be used to decrease the
cost of the insurance each year. These policies are in de-
mand, and many are now availing themselves of this form of
insurance in preference to all others.

J. S. CANTRALL,
General Special Agent.   Springfield, Ill.

E. D. GRISWOLD & SON
Mammoth · Department · Store

819-821 East Adams Street,

SPRINGFIELD, ILL.

Furniture, Stoves, Carpets. Curtains, Clocks, Lamps, Queensware, Art Gallery, Buggies, Harness, Saddles, Guns, Sporting Goods. Pumps, Hardware, Heavy Farm Machinery, Implements, Etc., Etc.

Road Wagons...............................$27.00 and up
Piano Box Buggies..........................40.00 and up
Buggy Poles with whipple trees and neck yoke, complete $3.50
Buggy Shafts, complete.......................... 2.50
Single Buggy Harness 4.75
Our Famous $12.50 Buggy Harness................. 9.90
Common No. 8 Cook Stoves....................... 7.75
Our Famous Borne Steel Range, size of oven, 20x22 inches, weight 700 lbs., high closet, porcelain or copper reservoir, and fuel bin.   Price.......... 35.00
Ladies' Solid Oak Sewing Rockers with brace arm, each .95
Expert Sewing Machines 14.90
Singer Sewing Machines......................... 19.90
E. D. Griswold & Son Sewing Machines........... 19.90
Buy one of our 95c Corn Shellers.

"Remember the Maine"
When you buy again.

E. D. GRISWOLD & SON
Adams Street bet. 8th and 9th.

Farmers National... Bank

SPRINGFIELD, ILLINOIS

✻

Capital,   -   -   -   -   -   - $200,000.00

Surplus and Undivided Profits,   -   110,000.00

✻

Receives Deposits and Loans Money on Approved Security . . . .

General Banking Business

✻

⇢ DIRECTORS ⇠

A HIGH-CLASS
BUSINESS SCHOOL
FOR BOTH
LADIES
AND
GENTLEMEN

LATEST
AND BEST
METHODS AND
APPLIANCES

NEW
TYPEWRITING
MACHINES

WRITE
FOR OUR
HANDSOME
ILLUSTRATED
CATALOGUE

H. B. CHICKEN, PRESIDENT

FOUR COURSES OF STUDY

BUSINESS COURSE
SHORTHAND COURSE
PENMANSHIP COURSE
PREPARATORY COURSE

ADDRESS
H. B. CHICKEN
SPRINGFIELD
ILLINOIS

The Continental

STRICTLY ONE PRICE ✌✌ TEL. 186 ✌✌ 120 EAST SIDE SQUARE

A Few

...Common Sense Reasons...
Why We Deserve Your Trade

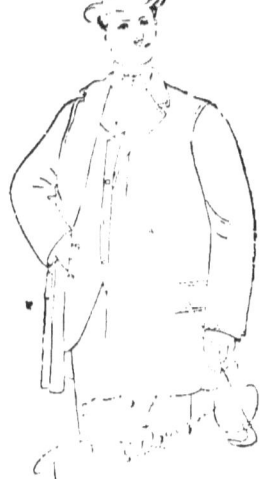

1. BECAUSE this is a new store and every article and every item in our vast establishment is new and up to date.

2. BECAUSE we operate five large stores in this and adjoining states.

3. BECAUSE we have one of the best-posted buyers in the market, who is always on the lookout for bargains.

4. BECAUSE buying as he does in large quantities gives us the advantage over small concerns, as our buyer is often able to dictate prices.

5. BECAUSE of our motto, A NIMBLE SIXPENCE IS BETTER THAN A SLOW SHILLING.

6. BECAUSE everything in our store is marked in plain figures and we sell at strictly one price to all, this not being a guess work store.

7. BECAUSE you are not taking any chances or depending on good luck when you buy here.

8. BECAUSE we have the best jointed store in Central Illinois.

9. BECAUSE if anything bought of us is not represented or does not give satisfaction, we check and we refund money without any why or wherefore.

10. BECAUSE we could give a thousand more good reasons, but the best reason of all is that you get the most for your money, and guaranteed to save you at least ten per cent on each purchase.

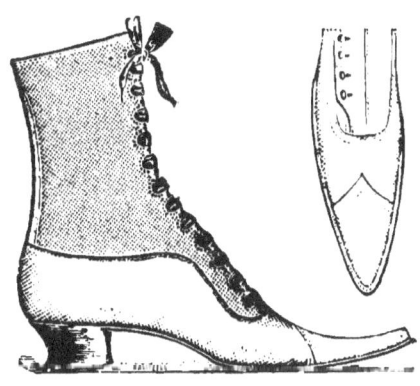

The Leading Furniture House of Central Illinois

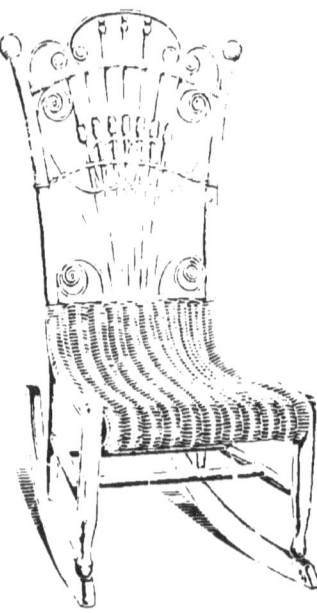

EUREKA COLLEGE

In the first rank of Col-
leges east or west

Courses Adapted to   Faculty Strong and
Every Department of Life   Enthusiastic

For Catalogue and Full Information, send to

J. H. HARDIN, Pres.

Eureka, Ill.

BIBLES

FINE STATIONERY

CARD CASES

POCKET BOOKS

WEDDING INVITATIONS

SCHOOL BOOKS

SUNDAY SCHOOL SUPPLIES

COE,
CARTER & COE
Leading
Booksellers & Stationers
N. W. Cor. 5th and Monroe Sts.
SPRINGFIELD,
ILL.

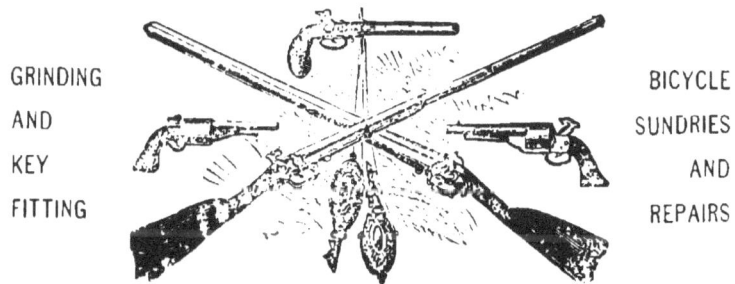

J. E. Klaholt

Dealer in

Diamonds ... Watches ... Jewelry
Clocks and Silverware

Spectacles Fitted by Expert Optician without extra charge

514 South Side Square **Springfield, Ill.**

ESTABLISHED 1838

"THE OLD RELIABLE"

DILLER'S DRUG STORE

WALLACE & DILLER
1838

ROLAND W. DILLER
1860

CORNEAU & DILLER
1849

ISAAC R. DILLER
1898

R. W. Diller, Veteran Druggist

122 SOUTH SIXTH ST. EAST SIDE SQUARE **SPRINGFIELD, ILL.**